'Fame doesn'

'What?'

'If I'd wanted you in my bed,' he drawled even more quietly, 'I would have invited you.'

Jenna jerked upright. 'I didn't *want* to be invited!'

'Then why were you groping around in my room?'

'I was looking for my bag!'

'In the middle of the night?'

'Yes! And what do you mean, fame doesn't rub off? You think I came because you're *famous*? *I* didn't ask for this! You kissed me...as though you *meant* it!'

Emma Richmond was born during the war in north Kent when, she says, 'farms were the norm and motorways non-existent. My childhood was one of warmth and adventure. Amiable and disorganised, I'm married with three daughters, all of whom have fled the nest—probably out of exasperation! The dog stayed, reluctantly. I'm an avid reader, a compulsive writer and a besotted new granny. I love life and my world of dreams, and all I need to make things complete is a housekeeper—like, yesterday!'

Recent titles by the same author:

A FAMILY CLOSENESS

THE LOVE TRAP

BY
EMMA RICHMOND

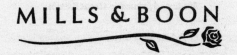

MILLS & BOON

*MILLS & BOON and the Rose Device
are trademarks of the publisher.
Harlequin Mills & Boon Limited,
Eton House, 18-24 Paradise Road, Richmond, Surrey TW9 1SR
This edition published by arrangement with
Harlequin Enterprises B.V.*

© Emma Richmond 1995

ISBN 0 263 79240 4

*Set in Times Roman 10½ on 12 pt.
01-9510-52950 C1*

Made and printed in Great Britain

CHAPTER ONE

Long, straight blonde hair spilling out over the end of the lounger, her lovely face tilted towards the sun, Jenna slowly opened bright blue eyes when she heard sundry crashing in the undergrowth at the end of the garden. Curious about anything and everything that was happening around her just lately, because she *needed* to be, she eased her aching left leg into a more comfortable position and turned to watch a man, a very attractive man, step out on to her lawn. Tousled brown hair, mirrored sunglasses, nice nose, firm mouth, a broad expanse of tanned chest, cut-off jeans, and a really terrific pair of long brown legs. The sort of man you met once in a lifetime ... Startled by such an oddly fanciful thought, Jenna hastily shut it away. He brushed himself off, eyed her appreciatively, gave a lazy smile, and began sauntering across the grass.

'Short cut,' he explained laconically.

'Right,' she agreed lamely.

'Don't mind, do you?'

'Not at all.'

He gave a vague sort of nod and squeezed himself between the villa wall and the garage, and disappeared.

Nice. And confident. Conceited? Probably. Good-looking men often were. David had been. Shut up, Jenna. With a despairing little sigh she idly contemplated a dip in the villa's small pool. She watched the sun's rays bounce off the gentle ripples, dazzling

5

prisms that beckoned invitingly if only she could find
the energy to accept. He'd seemed vaguely familiar,
as though she might have met him before, except she
knew that she hadn't. Perhaps she'd seen him around
the complex ... No, that wasn't right; he *reminded*
her of someone. Who?

Frowning slightly as the connection continued to
elude her, she was distracted by the sound of further
crashing in the undergrowth, and quickly turned her
head. If it was the intriguing man back ... No, not a
man, she saw as she turned her head, but a boy with
a shock of untidy brown hair, and she felt—relieved?
Or disappointed? But because she was a kind girl she
smiled as he slithered helplessly down the slope and
came to an eventual halt beside the pool. Sauntering
rather too nonchalantly across the grass to where she
lay, he gave a studiedly indifferent apology. 'Sorry. I
lost my balance.'

'Happens to us all,' she agreed with mock-
solemnity.

'Yeah.'

'Arm OK?'

He shook the plaster cast that covered one wrist as
though to test for breakages, and nodded. 'Yeah. It's
OK. I didn't mean to wake you up.'

'I wasn't asleep,' she denied. 'I was teleporting.'

He gave her a look of comic confusion, narrowed
his eyes as though trying to decide whether she was
pulling his leg, then grinned. Collapsing easily on to
the grass at her feet, he asked, 'Where'd yer go?'

'Middle Ages.'

'Yeah? Black Death and all that? Grim.'

'More along the lines of gallant knights and castle
procedure, I think.'

'Oh. I don't know much about the Middle Ages.' Leaning back, his good hand beneath his head, he stared up at the blue sky. 'Be neat, though, wouldn't it? If you could?'

'Providing no one could see you, or hear you, it would indeed. Where would you go?'

'Aw, I don't know. Spanish Main?'

'Pirate territory?'

'Yeah. Cap'n Morgan, Bluebeard... Can we go forward?'

Thinking about it for a minute, she shook her head. 'Nope, unlike time travel, for teleportation you have to have a point of reference, have to hold in your mind the image of where you want to be. Can't do that if no one's ever seen it, can you?'

'Oh. What about space?'

'Third crater on the left on the moon? Mmm,' she agreed consideringly, 'so long as you'd seen a photograph, or peered through a decent telescope with enough definition to be of use. You wouldn't be able to galaxy-hop, though.'

'Pity. Wouldn't it work with pure invention?'

'Certainly not,' she denied lazily. 'You might end up anywhere. It has to be entirely scientific and based on fact.'

'OK.' Closing his eyes, he snapped them open again and a look of disgust spread over his young face as someone yelled from near by.

'Mark!'

'Oh, nerd,' he muttered disgustedly, 'it's the dreaded Clarissa.'

'And who is the dreaded Clarissa?'

'My future grungy relative—if she has her way, that is. She's the pits! She whinged all the way down here,

moaned about the heat, and, if we had the car window
open, moaned that it blew her hair all over the place.
It wouldn't be so bad if she complained the same way
everyone else does! But she doesn't; she says things
like, "I'm really sorry to be such a nuisance..." And
now she's probably just discovered that I haven't un-
packed my things yet! And it doesn't have anything
to *do* with her!'

'Oh, dear. Deafness?' Jenna offered hopefully.

'Nah,' he denied. 'If I could hear you singing when
we arrived this morning—very badly,' he added with
another cheeky grin, 'then she sure can hear us talking.
And see us!'

'See us?' she echoed with a thoughtful glance towards the villas perched directly above them on the
hillside. 'Best not sunbathe topless, then, had I? And
no smart remarks, thank you.'

With a big sigh, he said glumly, 'She's as nice as
pie when the AP's around, and treats me as though
I'm retarded when he's not.'

'AP?' she queried.

'Aged Parent,' he grinned.

'Ah. And he tells you off for being rude...'

'AP does?' he exclaimed. 'No, not him, he never
tells anybody off! Just sort of looks at you—and you
find yourself telling him things you'd never *intended*
to tell him,' he confessed mournfully. 'And it isn't
fair, because he doesn't even know *why* he's looking
at you! He doesn't listen to what she says—or anyone
else,' he added with a grimace of mock-disgust. 'But
I have to!'

'Why?' she asked with a great deal of amusement.

'Because I'm *young*! And the young aren't allowed
to walk off when their elders are speaking to them.

And if they do, they get remarks like, ''It's a difficult age; one must make allowances...'' And if she disturbs the AP when he's busy, and it's my fault... I hate her!' he muttered.

'And show it. Not wise, my friend, not wise at all.'

'What?'

With a kind smile, she urged, 'Use psychology. Play her at her own game. Be oh, so nice, sweet, gallant...'

His puzzlement gave way to a very adult calculating look, and then he gave a slow smile. 'Yeah,' he breathed. 'Neat. That will drive her mad, won't it? Now why didn't I think of that?'

'Because you ain't as clever as me, of course.' And that wasn't a very wise thing to say, Jenna Draycott! That's meddling! Mmm, but having said it, impossible now to unsay it. Oh, well, if the dreaded Clarissa wasn't as bad as the boy made out, it might even work to everyone's advantage, mightn't it? A rift healed—and all thanks to Jenna Draycott, amateur psychologist. 'And if your aged parent doesn't even listen to her,' she continued lightly, 'then it isn't very likely that he'll be trapped into marriage, is it? I mean if he doesn't *hear* ...'

'Yes! But that's just it! He might get trapped into it without him even *realising*!'

'Oh, dear.'

When the shout was repeated, and the boy unwound himself with an ease she thoroughly envied, plaster cast or no, she stared up at him, then smiled at his obvious delaying tactics.

'What happened to the old guy with the bald head?'

'Uncle John? He's gone back to England.' Thank goodness, she mentally added. He'd insisted on driving her out to Spain; all very well-intentioned, but

absurd because, despite her gammy leg, she was perfectly capable of driving an automatic. Vague when
it suited him, slightly dotty, and if pointed in the right
direction usually quite happy, but as a driver? Forget
it; and she was now very determined that he would
never drive her anywhere ever again. She thought she
might even overcome her fear of flying if it came to
a straight choice.

'I heard him call you Tug,' he confessed with a
rather endearingly embarrassed air.

'Mmm, nickname. Apparently I used to tug on
people to gain their attention when I was small. I no
longer bother,' she added with a cheeky grin of her
own.

'Oh. Shall I call you that?'

'If you like. Or Jenna—or Hey, You! I answer to
most things.'

He gave a slow, extraordinarily appealing smile. Old
enough to know how to flirt, too young to do much
about it. Probably, she mentally qualified. On the
other hand, boys seemed to learn awfully young nowadays, and that from the ripe old age of twenty-six!
But she didn't feel twenty-six, she felt *old*, and decidedly disillusioned.

'Are you—um—here for long?' he asked a bit too
casually.

'A few weeks.'

'Neat, I——'

'Mark!' The voice was rasping, impatient.

With a despairing sigh, he muttered, 'Yeah, yeah,
I'm coming. Can I come down again?' he asked with
the air of one who pretended he didn't really care one
way or the other what the answer was.

'Sure, I'll probably be just lying around.'

'Teleporting,' he put in. Turning away, he flapped his hand, and Jenna watched him scramble up the steep slope towards his own villa. Nice boy, even if he did mangle the Queen's English so appallingly. And the sad thing was, she thought with a sigh, she probably would be just lying around. Forced into inactivity by the accident that had injured her leg, she was only slowly coming to terms with this enforced idleness. An idleness she was desperately pretending to enjoy. Although lying around on loungers for the whole of her stay, just to disguise her limp, did seem a bit excessive. It wasn't that she was defensive about it, or embarrassed—well, only insofar as people's curiosity went. Even when she simplified the explanation, for some reason people always wanted all the gory details! And to tell the truth, it would sound like boasting.

The problem was that Helen, who owned the villa and had kindly lent it to Jenna rent-free for as long as she wanted to use it, kept telling people how she had hurt her leg. Helen *boasted* about how Jenna had hurt her leg rescuing Helen's grandson from a coach crash, although she had promised Jenna faithfully that she hadn't told anyone here, or only the next-door neighbour, Peter, just in case Jenna should need any help, which wasn't really likely seeing as she had a maid who came in every day to do the shopping, the cleaning, even the cooking if she wanted her to.

Leaning back, determinedly trying to convince herself that this was what she wanted, that she was on holiday, that this was enjoyment, she gave a despondent sigh. She didn't even *like* lying in the sun, but if she went back home as white as she'd come out people would ask if she'd had bad weather, if she

hadn't enjoyed herself, because for some extraordinary reason people equated being brown with
having a good time. But, brown or not, at least she
looked better.

Raising her right hand, she thoughtfully admired
her long, painted nails, nails that up until the accident had, of necessity, been kept short. No sign now
either of the blisters, the pinches or the stains, which
were often the net result of working in wood and
fabric. A few weeks in hospital, and then conva-
lescing, had improved not only her hands, but her
whole appearance. She looked nothing like the scruff
budget she had become in recent years while helping
her father to lovingly restore the old furniture that
was their life. Now she looked rather elegant, idle, as
though she'd never done a day's work in her life—
the exact reverse of the truth, because she rarely ever
took a day off. She was no good at leisure, not this
sort anyway. She was one of those people who were
always busy, busy, busy, and she found this enforced
idleness unutterably frustrating.

Her sigh deepened; settling herself more
comfortably, very careful not to jar her injured leg,
promote the pain that hovered like an actor in the
wings just *dying* to come on, say his piece, she ad-
justed the black one-piece swimsuit that lovingly en-
cased her superb figure. Cut high, cut low, practically
backless, and an exhorbitant price for such a tiny piece
of material. But it had been a long time since she'd
spoilt herself, and she thought it worth every penny.
It made her feel good; slightly foolish, she admitted
wryly, but good, and feeling good was important at
the moment, even though there were few obvious signs
of there being anything wrong with her. Just a slight

indent in the calf of her left leg, and a long jagged scar on the sole of her foot, and the pain that swept without warning to darken her lovely eyes. And a limp, of course. And the nightmares. But it would get better. One day, it would be better, as nerve and muscle damage slowly healed . . . Shut up Jenna, don't think about it, she told herself.

Swinging her legs over the side of the lounger, she stood carefully, and heard the gentle slap of flip-flops come trundling through her garden from behind her. If a flock of camels, plus shepherd, had come trundling through her garden she didn't think she'd have been surprised. Resignedly turning her head, she stared at the same man she had viewed not half an hour earlier, and thoughtfully narrowed her eyes. Was *he* Mark's Aged Parent? she wondered in bemusement. They looked sufficiently alike for it to be a possibility, she suddenly realised. *Acted* alike, although not by any stretch of the imagination could he be called aged.

'You shouldn't frown,' he reproved lightly as he came to a halt beside her.

Glancing up, seeing her own reflection thrown back, she eased her frown, and commented without thinking, 'I can't see your eyes.'

Raising his hand, he removed the mirrored glasses. 'Better?'

'Yes.' Amusement lurked in the depths of eyes that were a bluey green and she felt her own mouth curve in response. An automatic reaction, impossible to resist. 'Mark is your son?' she queried softly.

He shook his head.

'Oh, but a relative of some sort?'

He nodded.

'And are you making another short cut?' Almost
appalled by the inanity of her remarks, she never-
theless found herself unable to dredge up anything
more intelligent. He was a very disturbing man, and
that was odd, because she would have sworn not half
an hour ago that no man would disturb her ever again.
Instant impact. Mesmerising. His air of stillness
perhaps, *waiting*. He shook his head again, and the
amusement in his eyes deepened, probably because
the helpless reaction of women was something he was
well used to.

'This is a visit?'

He gave an infinitesimal nod.

Jenna chuckled. Even if he *wasn't* Aged Parent, he
was definitely the sort of man the dreaded Clarissa
might want to pursue. A lot of other women too, no
doubt. But not herself. Easing the pressure on her bad
foot, unthinkingly using his shoulder to steady herself,
she forced herself to concentrate on a conversation
that was decidedly one-sided, and then couldn't remember where they'd got to. Ah, yes, Aged Parent.
The man who could make you confess with just a
look—that description could fit this man. Despite the
amusement, those eyes were definitely hypnotic. And,
although he appeared calm, amused, she sensed a
steely resolve lying just below the surface. Barely
visible, but certainly there. And if he was related to
Mark, as he'd said ...

Not even sure why she was bothering to sort out
her confusion, she glanced back at him, only to find
that he was watching her as carefully as she had been
watching him. His eyes still danced with amusement,
and she found she wanted to laugh out loud with the
sheer exuberance that this man engendered. It would

be good to laugh. It seemed an awfully long time since she had.

Her head tilted to one side, her long hair falling over one shoulder, she queried comically, 'Are you also related to Aged Parent?'

A fascinating little indent appeared beside his mouth and she felt an almost overwhelming desire to press her finger to it, touch it with her mouth, her tongue, and she gave a funny little shiver. Absurd. Utterly absurd.

'Mark is my brother,' he explained, and his voice was deep, rich, the sort of voice you could fall in love with without even *caring* what its owner looked like.

Somewhat bemused by her reaction, which, even allowing for all the dramas in her life of late, wasn't at all like her, she fought to pull herself together. Taking a deep determined breath, she exclaimed understandingly, 'Ah!' So, because of the disparity in their ages, their father must be quite elderly, hence the term Aged Parent. With a little nod of satisfaction, because she did so *hate* not to know things, she added, 'And you must be very like your father.'

'Must I?' he queried slowly. 'Why?'

'Because ... Well, because,' she stuttered lamely, and then gave an enchantingly helpless grin. 'I don't know,' she confessed. 'I think you are a very confusing man. Deliberately so?'

'Of course,' he agreed. 'It's called psychology.'

A startled look in her eyes, she opened her mouth, closed it again, then gave a rueful smile. 'He told you?'

'Of course. Mark tells me most things.'

A warning? Although Mark must have nipped round pretty smartly in order to tell him about *her*!
'And this visit is in the nature of——'

'Checking up on you? Yes.'

'To make sure I'm not a seducer of young boys?'

'Mmm . . . Or a bad influence—as sensualists often are,' he tacked on softly. Removing her hand from his shoulder, he gave it back to her, kissed the tip of her nose, and wandered away towards the bushes.

Sensualist? *Sensualist*? And had she passed muster? she wondered. Or failed? Not entirely sure whether to be annoyed or amused, she continued to stare after him. Did she *look* like a seducer of young boys? On the other hand, if she'd had a young sister and she'd come back with tales of meeting an older man . . .

That was the trouble with being fair-minded: you often saw the other person's point of view rather than your own. But sensualist? Staring down at herself, mouth pursed thoughtfully, she suddenly grinned. Better than being thought dowdy, wasn't it? And had he thought she was trying to interest *him*? Might be fun to try, because he was definitely intriguing. An intrigue he'd probably been practising for years. Cynic, she scolded herself, then sighed. A cool shower, she decided, a dim room, some relief from bright sunshine—and best take a pain-killer before she went out for the evening. An effort must be made, because she was sick to death of depression.

Making sure no one was around to see her, no more unorthodox visitors, she limped slowly inside to get herself a cold drink. The glass of fruit juice in her hand, she limped into the lounge and went to stand at the wide front window. Pushing it wide to admit the breeze, she gazed out. She didn't know this part

of Spain at all, but what she had so far seen she loved.
The warmth, the slowness, the smiles she had received, and if only the ache in her leg would go, if
only she could get about as she yearned to, if only
she could forget . . .

The villa was situated among a clutch of others nes-
tling in tall trees and palms, and from her vantage
point she could look out over the rest of the golf
complex. The very expensive and exclusive golf
complex, where the stars came to relax, where the rich
unwound. Stressed businessmen and women came to
get away from it all. Was her unknown visitor a
stressed businessman? A film star? Was that why he
seemed familiar? Maybe, and with a funny little smile
that she was quite unaware of playing about her mouth
she lingered a moment longer to admire the effect of
sunlight sparkling on a hundred pools, winking from
a thousand windows, warming the red roofs, turning
white walls into blinding perfection. White walls which
somewhere housed a man who might be a film star.

Her smile turning wry, she went to shower and
change.

Dressed in a long swirly skirt and matching top,
which would be cool, her hair wound on top of her
head in a rather strange-looking bun because she had
never quite got the hang of doing it properly, she drove
down the hill to the restaurant. Parking the car, she
walked slowly along one of the walkways to the central
square, where restaurants, bars and a couple of shops
surrounded the courtyard with its fountain, tables and
chairs which spilled from one restaurant to another.
Despite having only been on the complex for less than
a week, she was greeted like an old friend, given a
table, and waited on hand, foot and finger. Jenna

wondered how long it took for the real world to dis-
appear, for this to become the norm—or for ennui to
set in. Perhaps when you stayed here for months at
a time, as some of these people did, you never wanted
to go home.

Not in the least shy or nervous at being on her own,
and now that the pain was manageable, she forced
her troubles to one side, chatted with people at nearby
tables, smiled confidently at the one or two television
personalities that she spotted, and was somewhat
amused by her rather blasé, cosmopolitan air. As
though this were the way she lived; as though she had
hobnobbed with the rich and famous all her life. A
pretence, of course, but a necessary camouflage for
feelings which were still very raw.

When she had eaten, she retired to a high stool at
the bar, and because life had to be lived, because she
could be friendly and funny, and because she listened
to others, because she was pretty and not in the least
boring, and because she didn't do anything so obvious as ask for autographs, ask to have her photograph taken with this person or that, there were plenty
of people willing to talk to her, and flirt with her.
And when music from another bar grew louder,
swelled, filled the night with jazz, she idly began to
play an imaginary keyboard along the edge of the bar.
A young man near by grabbed some spoons, laughed,
and began to play them inexpertly. His girlfriend took
out tissue and comb and, with a little giggle, added
her contribution to the impromptu concert. Rising to
the challenge, Jenna swung fully round to face the
bar, flexed her fingers, shook her arms and began to
play 'properly'. The young barman grabbed a wooden
spoon and began tapping the optics in counterpoint,

and because it was a new game, something different, within minutes, others joined in using every imaginable prop possible as an instrument. Water jug, glasses, and a great deal of laughter as they gave a very credible accompaniment to the music floating out over the square.

People began to wander over from other bars to join in the party atmosphere as Jenna led her little group in one tune after another—and leaning in the archway watching her, near enough to touch, was the man who had strolled so casually through her garden.

CHAPTER TWO

HIS air of unconcerned assurance was—delightfully
disturbing. As was the memory of that light fleeting
kiss on her nose.

Jenna did a quick flourish with her right hand,
added the bass, and the man in the archway gave a
faint smile, looked down into his glass of wine, and
casually swirled the contents.

'You play very well,' her companion on the spoons
remarked.

'Thank you.'

'Been playing long?'

'Oh, years.'

'Steinway? Bechstein?'

'No, no, I only play tables.' With a great deal of
laughter, they swung nimbly into 'Bye Bye Blackbird'.

Julio, the head waiter, offered to make her enter-
tainment manager; Enrique, the golf pro, offered to
teach her golf, or tennis, or anything else she cared
to name. She raised her eyebrows, gave a slightly
wicked smile and, knowing very well that to go on
too long would make it boring, she crashed out the
final imaginary chords of the song, and picked up her
glass. Silently toasting her companions, and with a
graceful little bow to her applauding audience, she
turned to give Mark's brother a teasing look from the
corner of her eyes. He gave his slow smile, and perhaps
because she'd drunk a glass of wine on top of the

20

pain-killers, which she shouldn't have done, she felt
suddenly quite happy. And sensual.

'Hello again,' she greeted softly.

'Hello.' His voice was equally soft, but far more
disturbing than her own could ever be.

'How's Mark?' Original, Jenna.

'I believe—teleporting.' And he smiled—a wide
smile that crinkled his eyes, and stupidly made Jenna's
pulse accelerate. He was also obviously someone who
never promoted conversation, merely answered what
he was asked as economically as possible, which might
make it very difficult to indulge in even the idlest of
social intercourse. Advancing and rejecting in her
mind such blindingly original questions as, How long
are you here for? Do you swim, play golf...? she
looked down into her own drink and gave a helpless
chuckle.

'You're doing fine,' he praised with great solemnity
belied by the twinkle in his eyes. A twinkle that held
just the tiniest trace of cynicism. Why?

'And how fine are you doing?' she quipped.

'Oh, as always.'

Which meant, what? 'Do you...?' she began, and
then stopped because she could see that she no longer
had his attention. He was staring beyond her and,
although the dawning expression on his face could
not quite be called horror, it was as near to it as he
probably got. He switched his eyes back to her, saluted
her with his glass and disappeared through the
archway.

Turning to see what had caused the horror, she
watched a large lady, dressed in a rather strange-
looking caftan, press determinedly through the crush,
her eyes fixed firmly on the archway. As she passed

Jenna, she quickened her pace. Amused, Jenna turned back to Enrique, and saw wicked laughter glittering in his dark Spanish eyes as he too watched the progress of the determined lady.

'She will not succeed,' he commented with a wide engaging smile. 'He is much too wily.'

'You know him well?'

'But of course, he comes here often, to play the golf—at which he is very good—or the tennis, or to do whatever it is he does when he is not being pursued by many, many women.' Turning to Jenna, he grinned. 'You too?'

She shook her head. 'I'm much too lazy.' Which was as good an answer as any, she supposed. Certainly she couldn't pursue him physically. Not at the moment anyway, and even if she could she wouldn't; nothing worse than chasing after a man who didn't want to be chased. Or even a man who did, she thought, her face sobering, and then changed his mind—like David. David, who had been unable to cope with the trauma of her accident. *He* had been unable to cope. Love? That had been no sort of love at all. Good-looking, decisive, arrogant, she supposed, and he'd declared his undying love for her—until the accident. And on top of everything else the rejection had come so very hard.

She'd had a couple of previous relationships that had started out in hope, on her side anyway, and ended in disillusionment. Her own fault probably, perhaps because she expected too much, but, even if that was so, she'd been determined not to compromise. David hadn't felt like a compromise. It had felt like the real thing: enduring. With a bitter little smile, she quickly finished her drink.

She had wanted to be married, had wanted a husband who would adore her to the exclusion of all else, someone she could adore in return. Someone who didn't pretend. She'd thought David didn't pretend—then had found out differently. He'd pretended to like what she liked because he thought it would please her; when the test had come, he'd been unable to pretend any more—and she'd felt betrayed.

Determinedly pushing away the self-pity, she realised that for sanity's sake she had to put it all behind her, get on with her life, which, as soon as she was fit again, would hopefully take up all of her time and energy. Not only helping Dad in the furniture-restoration business, but running her little dance school. And hopefully, one day, someone else would come along to give her the love she needed, the love she needed to return. But not yet. Not for a long time yet. Although, as her mother was so fond of pointing out, 'Love doesn't wait to be asked, and, when it does come, there ain't nothing you can do about it. He probably won't be your ideal, probably won't be anything like you thought you wanted, but, warts and all, if you love, you love unequivocally.' The way she had with David?

Beginning to feel tired now, not quite used to the late hours everyone kept here, she got carefully to her feet, smiled and waved her goodbyes, and walked slowly back to her car. It was a warm, clear, beautiful night, a night made for love, and she hastily blinked back stupid tears. Halting, she took a deep breath, inhaled the scents from the fragrant flowers that lined the walkways, listened to the animated chirping of the cicadas, told herself that she was alive, lucky to be so, young, a lot of life to be lived yet, and one day

she would look back on this interlude and laugh.
Yeah? And please God tonight let me sleep, not lie
wakeful and in pain, she pleaded silently.

Opening her eyes, she continued towards her car,
then halted again. The man, whose name she still did
not know, was leaning against the passenger door,
watching her, his glass of wine still held in one hand.
Don't be daft enough to fall in love with him, will
you, Jenna? No, not even rebound stuff. Then she
fleetingly wondered how you know you ever had a
choice. With a wry smile, she continued slowly towards him.

He gave a crooked grin. 'Going my way?'

Without answering, she opened the car door, waved
him inside and took her place behind the wheel. They
didn't speak as she drove them back up the hill, but
it wasn't a constrained silence—it was comfortable,
soothing almost. When she pulled into her driveway
they sat for a moment just watching each other and,
much to her surprise, despite her warnings to herself,
there was definitely a leap of excitement, an acknowledgement, an odd little feeling of—hope.

He gave his slow smile and ordered softly, 'Tell me
about you. Tell me why you're in Spain, how long
you intend to stay, where you've been, what you've
done.'

Feeling warm and sleepy, she leaned her cheek
against the head-rest and murmured, 'I don't even
know your name.'

'You don't?'

She shook her head, and wondered at the disbelief
in his smile.

'Bay.'

'Bay? As in watch? View? Window?'

'Don't be facetious,' he reproved lightly. 'As in Bayne Rawson.'

'Different.'

'Mmm. Begin.'

'Don't you want to know mine?'

'I already know it. Stop prevaricating. Begin.'

Somewhat amused by his orders, and with no real desire to go in, try to court sleep that usually proved so elusive, she quipped lightly, 'In the past week, I have been driven from St Malo to Bilbao, from Burgos to Madrid, and because my chauffeur, my uncle John, still thinks thirty miles per hour excessive we arrived in the ancient city in the dark, and were unable to find our hotel. Because Madrid is huge, because the roads, even at night, are incredibly busy, and because my trusty street map didn't seem to bear any relation to the actual streets, we hijacked a taxi driver to lead us, only to discover that we had booked into a hotel in the busiest part of the city and that we had to park in an underground car park definitely reminiscent of an ancient tomb. It was also extremely humid, the hotel did not have air-conditioning, neither did it have a bar, the restaurant closed at nine o'clock and, on the rare occasions it was open, was a definite clone of Fawlty Towers. You are familiar with Fawlty Towers?'

'I am.'

'Good. And on the only occasion we ventured to eat there we were hurled at a table, given a bottle of indifferent red wine, soup we had not ordered, dry rolls. If you laid your spoon down for even a fraction of a second, your soup plate was whisked away, replaced by the main meal, which was yanked away from you if you so much as paused, and then replaced by a dish of ice-cream. Coffee was not offered and, before you could ask, your chair was pulled from beneath you and you were halfway down the corridor without any clear idea of how you had got there—along with fourteen Japanese nuns who'd had the misfortune to be directed there for dinner by their tour operator.'

He chuckled. 'Unfortunate, because there are some truly excellent hotels in Madrid. I will allow for exaggeration,' he added with a magnanimous little inclination of his head.

'Thank you.'

'You are entirely welcome. Please continue.'

She gave an involuntary chuckle. How nice to meet someone who understood *perfectly*, because, of course, she had exaggerated and, despite the hotel staff being under pressure, they had been courteous—hastily courteous, she mentally corrected, and had laughed when she'd gently teased them about it. 'Undaunted,' she continued happily, 'because we are well-travelled, you understand, and used to eccentricities, the following morning, determined to enjoy other untold delights of Madrid, we sauntered out to sightsee.'

'On foot? In the hottest August on record? When the humidity was higher than anyone can remember?'

'Er, no. Not on foot. Uncle John is old, I am lazy, so we hired a taxi for the day and drove to all the places that we thought we would actually like to get out and see one day.'

'A sort of advance recce?'

'Exactly. We saw the palace, the railway station, the Prado, the cathedral, the old quarter. The taxi-driver kindly drove very slowly along the exclusive shopping street....'

'Serrano?'

'Yes. You know Madrid?'

'I do.'

'So I definitely need to go back one day to see it all properly. All I've had so far are tantalising glimpses of the Prado Museum, which I particularly wanted to see, and which is supposed to be excellent ...'

'It is.'

'And the palace, which looked magnificent... And oh, so many things,' she added wistfully.

'Then next time go in March or October, when it's cooler,' he advised. 'And then where?'

'Well, Uncle John was hot, couldn't sleep for the heat, so we decided to head for Toledo, or Segovia, or Avila ...'

'Only he was driving,' he smiled, 'so you didn't.'

'No, we came straight here, by a roundabout route,' she grinned, 'because we got lost, several times! And I am never going to allow him to drive me again!'

'Why *did* you allow him to?' he asked quizzically. 'Don't you like driving?'

After an infinitesimal pause, she declared, 'I *adore* driving.'

'Good. Then you can drive me—to Albacete.'

With a blink of astonishment, she asked lamely, 'You don't drive?'

'Yes, but seeing as Mark was quite insistent that I invite you, you may as well be useful.'

'*Mark* insisted?'

'Mmm. Biological urges are hell at his age, aren't they?'

'I don't know,' she denied helplessly. 'Are they?'

'Yes. So don't lead him on just because you can, will you? If you do need to practise your flirting techniques, use me. You do *know* the rules?' he asked softly.

Rules... Ah. About to tell him exactly what she thought of his assumptions, and that flirtation was the last thing she wanted, she suddenly changed her mind. Why not? What harm would it do? And mightn't it be the very thing to take her mind off her own troubles? He was attractive, amusing, experienced, her mind whispered, but she was in no danger; he was definitely not the sort of man to force a woman, and it might be fun to pay him back for his misconceptions. Rather insulting misconceptions that she would deliberately hurt a young boy.

'I know *some* rules,' she qualified demurely. 'Yours differ, do they?'

'No.'

A twitch to her lips, she murmured, 'How un-equivocal. I have rules too.'

'I thought you might.'

With a little choke of laughter, beginning to enjoy herself hugely, she queried, 'And how long would this trip take?'

'A couple of hours.'

Time enough for mischief, if that was what was on his mind. Conjuring up a mental picture of the map, she frowned. 'I don't recall seeing the name.'

He kindly spelt it for her. 'A-l-b-a-c-e-t-e.'

Her frown cleared, and she smiled. 'That's how you pronounce it—Albachetty?'

'Mmm. La Mancha country, well worth seeing.'

'La Mancha?' she asked in delight. 'Don Quixote?'

'Mmm. Yes? No?'

'I'll think about it.'

'Don't take too long.' With another smile, a smile that was beginning to fascinate her, because it wasn't *exactly* friendly, he sipped from his glass and then ordered her to do the same.

Amused, she did so. Then he leaned forward, lightly licked the wine from her lips, and an odd little spiral of excitement ran through her.

'Always better with the taste of expensive wine,' he informed her. 'But then, you know that, don't you?'

'Do I?'

'Yes.' There was a husky note in his voice that she suspected was deliberate but, even so, would probably undermine the resistance of the hardest heart, and Jenna's certainly wasn't that, no matter how hard she'd been trying. 'Thanks for the lift,' he added with the same disturbing inflexion. Opening his door, he climbed out, waggled his fingers at her, merged with the shadows, and disappeared.

Touching hesitant fingers to her mouth, she continued to stare at the spot where he had disappeared. Calculated behaviour. Gentle warnings delivered with studied charm. Well, two could play at that game. Thought she was a Delilah, did he? A Delilah who liked expensive wine. Then Delilah was what he'd get. Certainly she was totally fed up with being herself.

Just don't try and make him pay for David's behaviour, will you? a little inner voice warned. No, she wouldn't do that; of course she wouldn't. A moment of uncertainty darkened her lovely eyes, then she dismissed it. *He* was the one who'd started it. And you're experienced enough to finish it, are you? she asked herself. She dismissed that as well—because she knew very well she wasn't. Climbing out, she went inside.

Lying in bed, she continued to think about him. Laconic, amusing, different—and definitely with a trace of cynicism. And he thought her a butterfly. An immoral one at that, probably. Just because she was blonde and had the sort of looks that men found attractive? Yet the memory of his tongue touching her lip was . . . disturbing, as were the erotic visions it now conjured up. Erotic visions that wore David's face— but Bayne Rawson's bluey green eyes.

Go to sleep, Jenna.

She woke at four, as she so often did, despite the pain-killer she'd taken before going to bed. There was a nagging ache that felt as though someone was scraping the very marrow from her bones, burrowing behind her knee, and the only thing that seemed to work was to get up, limp around, curse it, cry, get angry, miserable, and take another pain-killer. And she was so *tired* of it. All very well for the doctor to say it would take a few months—she still had to get through those months!

Returning to bed an hour later, she thankfully fell into a deep sleep, but on waking the memory of it was still there, an impression of pain if not the pain itself. And all this being cheerful in the face of adversity was extraordinarily wearing. Perhaps it had been a mistake to come. She might have been better among family and friends, people who *knew*. No, she mentally denied, pity she could not take. She also regretted her behaviour with Bay the night before. It had been foolish, not only to give him the wrong impression of herself, but to allow him to think she would go to Albacete with him. In the cold light of day she knew she could never carry it off. She wasn't a flirt, wasn't sure she knew how to be. Well, no real harm done; she would just tell him no when she saw him.

Forcing herself to eat some toast, she assembled her bits and pieces on the lawn—and no sooner had she got comfortable than Mark arrived.

'Hi, Tug.'

'Hi, yourself.' Remembering Bay's strictures of the night before, she carefully refrained from saying or doing anything that might be misconstrued, which wasn't easy, because she didn't know *what* might be misconstrued. Eyeing the cast on his arm, which was getting progressively grubbier, she smiled at him. 'How's the dreaded Clarissa?'

'Don't know. She's gone up to Barcelona for a few days so I haven't had a chance to try out the new psychology.' Collapsing on to the grass as though he was exhausted, he added with the callousness of youth, 'She probably thinks absence will make the heart grow fonder or something. Got anything to drink?'

Passing across the Thermos of orange which she had brought out to save frequent trips inside, she offered, 'Help yourself.'

'Thanks.' Taking a healthy swig, he rested it on his crossed knees. 'Seen Aged Parent?'

'Nope. I *yearn* to,' she grinned, 'but no, sadly he has not been among the army who currently march through my garden.'

'Oh.' Obviously not particulary bothered, he asked instead, 'Got any knitting needles?'

Staring at him, trying to gauge what on earth he wanted knitting needles for, she shook her head. 'Might I ask why you want them?'

He held up his cast. 'Itches.'

'Ah. Have a look in the wardrobe in the downstairs bedroom at the back of the villa; you'll probably find a metal coat-hanger. Strong young lad like you could probably straighten one out...'

'Yeah. Neat.' Handing her back the flask, he wandered into the villa—and with almost perfect timing the bushes parted and his brother emerged. He was bare-chested, and an old pair of jeans clung lovingly to his narrow hips. Amusement still lurked in his eyes and around his mouth as he moved lazily towards her, and she felt an odd little frisson of excitement in her tummy. Squashing it, determined to be sensible, she arranged her face into a polite mask, but it didn't stop the feelings. This man *bothered* her, and she didn't want to be bothered.

He halted beside her, collapsed on to the grass as though equally exhausted as his young brother, then gave a slow smile. 'Coffee?'

'If you make it.'

He nodded without apparent surprise, uncoiled himself and went inside. Minutes later he was back with two coffees. He handed her one, then sat cross-legged on the grass, coffee-cup nursed in his palms. 'You were aware, were you,' he asked lazily, 'that someone was rummaging around in your villa?'

'Mmm, your brother. He's looking for a coat-hanger.'

'Ah.' He didn't ask why his brother wanted one. Perhaps he knew. Perhaps it was all a carefully laid out plan. Whatever it was, she had to make it clear that she wasn't the sort of person he thought she was, and that casual friendliness was *all* she had in mind. And that she wouldn't go to Albacete, of course.

About to do so, she was thwarted when Mark wandered out. He seemed quite unsurprised to see his brother lounging there, and vaguely waved the coat-hanger he'd found. 'Hi, unbend this for me, will you?'

'Sure.' Taking the coat-hanger, he easily unbent it and handed it back.

'Not bad for an aged parent,' he murmured as he inserted one end into his cast and wiggled it about a bit, then gave a blissful sigh. 'Excellent! This is Tug, by the way. She wanted to meet you.'

'She did?' he asked with lazy amusement. 'I thought she already had.'

Staring at him, her face mirroring her confusion, she demanded, '*You're* Aged Parent? But you said Mark was your brother.'

'He is. Aged Parent, or, to give it its correct title, Aged Parent Substitute is the derogatory and quite unfair, not to say insulting—term he uses for me.'

'Mum and Dad died when I was a baby,' Mark explained airily, 'so he had to give up his all in order to bring me up.'

'Ah, that would, of course, account for his air of deprivation,' she agreed sagely. 'Work all night, did he, so that he could be free to look after you in the day?'

'Yep.'

'Went without just to give you a good start in life?'

'Yep.'

'Continuing guilt trip?'

'Yeah. Sad, ain't it?'

'Tragic,' she agreed.

Mark laughed and whacked his brother on the back. 'See? I told you she was neat.'

'I don't know about neat—wretched would be more like it,' Bay complained, 'expecially when I've spent the last thirteen years trying to convince you how much you owe me. Go on, scat, you're cramping my style.'

'Didn't know you had one!' With a grin Mark skipped out of his brother's lazily reaching arm, then scuffed awkwardly at the grass. 'Did you—um—ask her yet?'

'I did.'

'Neat.' Obviously restored to energy once more, he loped across the grass and shoved his way through the bushes at the end of the garden.

Fighting not to be charmed by the pair of them, Jenna drawled with mild sarcasm, 'How very like you he is.'

Bay raised one eyebrow.

'The immediate assumption that an invitation only has to be issued and it will be accepted with delight. I hadn't said that I would go.'

'Call him back,' he ordered lazily.

'And lose his budding adoration?' He narrowed his eyes, and she smiled. 'Just testing. He's a nice boy.'

'Yes. I'd like to keep it that way.'

'So I gathered. I don't need to be hit over the head with a point.'

'Good. He's at an impressionable age.'

'Unlike his brother.'

'Mmm. You intend to lead *me* astray?'

'Could I?'

'No.'

'Not the way you lead all the young ladies on the complex astray?' she asked sweetly. 'Because it hadn't quite escaped my notice how women keep following *you* around. Are you a good catch or something?'

'Mmm.'

'About to be engaged?' she probed.

He looked vaguely alarmed. 'Am I? I don't recall proposing to anyone.'

'The dreaded Clarissa?' she prompted.

'Clarissa?'

Staring at him, her head on one side, she frowned. Judging by his tone, that was another warning. Forcing a light tone, she quipped, 'Well, I dare say if you can't even remember who she is you can't be going to marry her, can you?'

'No. Whose turn is it to make coffee?'

'Yours.'

'Didn't I just make it?'

'Mmm.'

'Then it's a good job we aren't a couple.'

'It's no doubt unwise of me to ask, but why?'

'Because we're both so laid-back we'd never do anything, would we?'

'Would we want to?'

'Probably not. But we aren't a couple, are we? Nor likely to be,' he tacked on softly.

'No,' she agreed. 'And neither are you laid-back.' He raised one eyebrow in simulated surprise, and she gave a slow, hopefully derisive smile. 'Controlled— and utterly calculating. Aren't you?'

'Am I?'

'Yes. Which brings us to——'

'Albacete,' he completed, as though he could easily read minds. 'And you won't get those lovely long legs brown by keeping a towel over them.'

'True. But by the same token I don't want to get those lovely long legs burnt, do I? About Albacete...'

'Yes? You have half an hour.'

'Half an hour?' she repeated foolishly.

'To get ready.' Rising to his feet, he lifted a languid hand, drifted over to the bushes and made the same unorthodox exit his brother had.

'But I'm not going to Albacete,' she called after him. Was she? And yet going to Albacete would be something to do. Had to be better than lying here getting roasted. And he *amused* her. Made her feel alive. Crossing swords was really rather exhilarating. And it would be nice to teach him a little lesson in assumptions, wouldn't it?

Determinedly squashing the little voice in her head that told her not to be a fool, that she would be biting off a great deal more than she could chew, she gathered up her bits and pieces and slowly made her way inside. Lightly making up her face, she brushed her hair, changed into a white skirt and navy and white striped top, checked that she had her pain-killers in her bag, decided she would have to do, and went to wait for him on the front path.

CHAPTER THREE

YOU'RE mad, Jenna scolded herself, to go off with someone you don't even know. Yes. But people on the complex knew him... And Bay had made it very clear... Made what very clear? she asked herself impatiently. He'd warned her about leading his brother astray, warned her about trying to lead *him* astray— but she was so very fed up with being sensible.

Still mentally debating the whole issue, comforting herself that it was only for a few hours, that they weren't going very far, she heard the sound of an approaching car and looked up as a rather battered Citroën pulled in to the kerb. The passenger door was shoved open, and without further time to think she climbed in, smiled at Mark sitting in the back seat, and fitted her seatbelt into place.

'I thought I was to drive.'

'You are. Later.'

Noting the clean jeans and blue shirt he'd changed into, noting that he *noticed* her noting, and refusing to give him the satisfaction of thinking she cared, she turned casually away, idly reached for the book lying on the parcel shelf in front of her, and gave a little blink of shock. Peeping sideways, aware that he still watched her, cynical humour on his face, she stared back at the book.

Native Land by Bayne Rawson. *This* Bayne Rawson? Had to be. Her movements slow, almost clumsy, she turned the hardback book over, and his

amused face stared back. *That* was why he'd seemed
familiar: she must have seen his picture on a book-
jacket somewhere. To gain time, try to unscramble
her thoughts, she flipped up the cover and ran her
finger down the list of previous books that he'd
written. Staring at the last title, *Nowhere To Go*, she
blinked in astonishment. She'd *read* that on the ferry
coming over! And that, of course, was why he'd
thought she must know his name. His smile of disbelief had been because he was *famous*! Oh, good
grief, did that mean he thought that was why she'd
been nice to his brother? Life was just so full of un-
expected pitfalls.

Eyeing him just a little bit nervously, she blurted,
'I didn't know.'

'So I gather.'

'But you thought I did. Didn't you?'

'Mmm.'

'Thought I was chasing you.'

'*Cultivating* me,' he corrected her as he finally set
the car in motion.

'Because people do?'

'Sometimes. Sometimes they just ask a lot of daft
questions.'

'Oh,' she mumbled thoughtfully. 'Is that what the
large lady in the bar was doing? Chasing you in order
to ask daft questions?'

'Mmm. She thought I would be ideal to give a talk
to her women's club in Hampshire. And although I
am delighted and grateful that people buy my
books...'

'That doesn't necessarily mean that you have the
desire, or the inclination, to give talks on them.'

'No.'

'I'm sorry,' she apologised again with a rueful grimace. 'You must have thought me an idiot, not recognising you...'

His eyes widened, and he flicked her an amused glance as he slowed at the next junction. 'Now why on earth would I think you an idiot? Do you suppose me to be one of those people who court attention? Want to be fêted, recognised wherever they go? I promise you I'm not. I'm certainly not about to get on my high horse, sulk...'

'Not a prima donna?' she smiled.

'Look a bit silly, wouldn't I?'

'Yes.'

'Can we go now?'

'What? Oh, yes, sorry,' she apologised as she realised they were still hovering at the exit on to the main road. So what did he think now? Now that he knew she hadn't known? That she was naturally friendly? Flirted with anything in trousers? Or that she was attracted to him? A subject best left alone, she decided.

'Not going to behave differently towards me, are you?' he asked quietly.

'Differently?' she asked, genuinely perplexed. 'No, why should I?' She might be a bit nervous of going off on a trip with him, but that wasn't because he was an author. It was because he was a man. A very attractive and disturbing man.

'Because people do,' he said simply.

Yes, she had seen the way some of the people at the compelx had behaved towards the better known of the celebrities, and she gave a wry smile because she knew that when she went home she would in all probability boast about having met him. He became quite a friend of mine, she could say casually, then chuckle softly to herself.

And why, she wondered whimsically, were authors so fêted, when furniture restorers were ignored? They had a talent, certainly, much as most people had talents, the only difference being in their variety. She couldn't cobble a decent sentence together and Bayne probably couldn't bang in a nail—a fact that diminished neither of them. But it did alter things a bit, didn't it, despite her denial? He might have joked about not chasing him, but it had still been a warning, and that made it difficult to know how to behave. A few weeks ago it wouldn't have been a problem, but because of David, who'd knocked her confidence in herself as a woman for six, she wasn't quite sure how to behave. She needed a friend, someone to talk to, someone to take her mind off her troubles—but not a lover, not an affair, and certainly no complications.

But then, he didn't want that either, did he? So what did he want? Merely to make sure she didn't lead his brother astray? Or to indulge in a little light flirtation because he thought she knew the rules?

A slightly troubled frown in her eyes, she asked interestedly, 'Are you here to write a book?'

'I am. And this is in the nature of research.'

'Oh, good. What are we researching?'

'Descriptions of countryside. You may wield the camera,' he offered as he nodded towards the small camera on the passenger ledge.

'Ah. *That's* why you allowed your brother to invite me.'

'Mmm,' he agreed blandly, 'Mark being unable to do so at present because of his wrist.'

'Yes, how foolish of me not to have thought of that myself.'

'Mmm.'

Her smile slightly forced, and doubting that it had anything whatever to do with photography, but rather wishing that she did know what it had to do with, she exchanged book for camera. 'Now?' she asked drily.

'Now,' Bay agreed. 'Just general shots so that when I come to write I can at least see what I'm writing about. Mark will make notes on the map. Picture one is such and such, and so on.'

Turning to smile at Mark as he moved forwards to lean his arms—well one arm and one plaster—along their seats, she teased, 'You've been very quiet.'

'Yeah. I was tracing the route.' Holding out the folded map, he showed her, then settled back in his seat and got out his pen. He obviously took research very seriously.

'I've read one of your books,' she said quietly as she took a picture of the foothills through which they were passing. 'I just didn't remember who it was who wrote it.' Then she wondered if that had been boasting, or fawning, and wished she hadn't said anything.

'Which one?'

'*Nowhere to Go.*'

'Buy it?'

Slightly puzzled, she shook her head. 'Well, Uncle John did. On the ferry coming over,' she added as though the point might need clarifying.

He flicked her a look from the corner of his eyes, and gave his slow smile. 'Good,' he approved.

'Probably foolish of me to ask, but why?'

'Royalties, of course. Don't get 'em if you borrow the book, do I?'

'Oh.'

'Quite. How else am I to support my expensive lifestyle? Enjoy it?'

'Yes, very much. A bit violent,' she commented, 'but enjoyable. I liked your hero.'

'Good.'

Resting the camera on her knee, she glanced at him again. He still wore the faint smile round his mouth, slightly cynical, but still a smile, and he still disturbed her, she found. But, because she was no longer sure of her judgement where men were concerned, she tried to dismiss it. Tried to ignore the little ache she felt when she looked at him.

Just a man, Jenna, she told herself. Wealthy, attractive, possibly arrogant, and definitely cynical. But then, she'd been pretty cynical herself of late. And he was clever, she added to herself. The book had been a political thriller set in Turkey, she remembered, and she had been very impressed by his imagination, his use of words. So why on earth hadn't she remembered who had written it? Because she read so many books? Because it was the first one of his that she'd read? Or because her mind had been on her own problems and everything else stayed on the periphery of her vision? Uncle John had enjoyed it too, said it had been damned clever, so perhaps, after all, writers were more worthy of being fêted than humble furniture restorers, because, although you needed some imagination, a bit of artistic ability, you didn't need complicated, clever plots.

'Camera?' he prompted softly.

With a little start, she obediently raised it and took several more snaps as they drove through the last of the foothills. She recorded, for posterity, small villages, hamlets, isolated farmhouses. Slowly, the scenery began to change, grow more and more desolate. Once through Tobarra, she stared in astonishment at the wide, dusty plain that spread seemingly unendingly before them. And, although she had been aware of the build-up of warmth as the sun rose towards its zenith, all of a sudden heat seemed to batter them from all sides, dull the senses. Yet also, for some odd reason, it seemed to heighten perception, and the contrast from rolling hills to sun-scorched earth was dazzling.

Heat haze danced across the flat ground towards the horizon, shimmering in the still air. Raising the camera again, she took several shots, tried to encompass all that he might need.

'You almost expect a lone horseman to canter slowly into view,' she observed softly as she continued to stare at the totally inhospitable terrain. 'Hat pulled low over a half-smoked cigar, a poncho concealing his guns.'

'The man with no name?' Bay asked lazily.

'Mmm, didn't they make the films in Spain?'

'I believe so—might even have been here. I think I even recognise that ruined farmhouse,' he chuckled.

'Who's the man with no name?' Mark demanded.

'Clint Eastwood. Spaghetti westerns?' she offered in amusement when he continued to look puzzled. '*The Good, the Bad and the Ugly*?'

'Oh, those,' he commented dismissively.

Bay grinned. 'If it doesn't have a Ninja turtle...'

'Bay!' Mark protested. 'That's kid's stuff!'

'Oh, sorry,' he apologised meekly.

Turning to give Mark a commiserating smile, Jenna stared through the rear windscreen at the dust that had been disturbed by their passing. Reds, ochres, brown, everything burnt by the relentless sun. It had been such a long, hot, dry summer, not only here, but over most of Europe. In pleasant surroundings— a town or small village—it wasn't so noticeable, but here there was stark reminder of what drought could do. Or was it always like this? Certainly it was far removed from what tourists normally saw. A far cry from the Costa del Sol. But better, oh, how much better, despite the heat. 'How far are we from the Sierra Nevada?' she asked curiously.

'Not so far,' Bay informed her. 'Show her on the map, Mark.'

Obediently handing the map across, Mark leaned over her shoulder to see, then pointed eagerly. 'There!'

She glanced at the high ridge shown on the map, then let her eye wander across the creased and battered page. Granada, Almería, then, further across, Sevilla, Córdoba—wonderful names, names to conjure with, names that rolled off the tongue. Working out distances, she promised herself that she would take the time to go that way before she went home. Maybe not as far as Córdoba, but certainly Granada, up to Linares, bypassing Madrid and on up to Guadalajara, then Zaragoza, Andorra maybe; she'd always wanted to go there...'

'Camera?' Bay prompted softly.

'Oh, sorry,' she apologised quickly. Returning the map to Mark, she picked up the camera and hastily took a few more shots. There was hardly any other traffic on the road, and breaking down out here would certainly be no joke. She glanced surreptitiously at the petrol gauge and temperature dial.

As though aware of what she was doing, he flicked her a glance. 'Calculating men,' he informed her blandly, 'never forget petrol.'

'Good.' Had that rankled? That she'd called him calculating? She had no idea. And he wasn't only calculating, but laconic. Not that he was terse, more deliberately bland, hiding—what? 'Mmm?'

'La Mancha,' he repeated.

'What?' she asked, startled. 'Is this it?'

'Mmm,' he confirmed as he waved one hand to encompass their surroundings.

Delighted, her musings forgotten, she stared about her with fresh eyes, tried to conjure up mental pictures. Had Cervantes trodden this dusty plain? Scribbled notes, much as Bay would no doubt do? Blowing damp hair off her forehead, Jenna glanced at him, and smiled. No Cervantes this, nor Don Quixote either. He didn't even look hot and uncomfortable in the fierce heat. In fact, he looked remarkably relaxed, one elbow resting in the open window, his strong hands relaxed on the wheel. His mirrored sunglasses hid his eyes, and his dark hair was tousled attractively by the humid air which not so much blew through the open window as heaved, like lumpy soup. Amused by her analogy, she began to sing softly one of the songs from the hit musical *Man of La Mancha*—'To Dream the Impossible Dream'.

Bay gave his slow smile, and joined in. Unfortunately, neither of them could remember more than the first verse, and after having mangled it thoroughly they switched to the title song, which had a much more rousing beat and was definitely suitable for singing in cars.

'Hey, that's pretty good,' Mark complimented.

'Thank you,' Bay said drily.

'So, who's this Keyhotey fellow?'

'Mark!' Bay reproved. 'Don't they teach you anything at that fancy school of yours? Don Quixote! Cervantes!'

'Still never heard of him,' he grinned.

'Windmill tilter?' Jenna prompted.

'Windmills?' he snorted in astonishment. 'What windmills? There aren't any!'

'Metaphoric ones,' Bay murmured with an irrepressible laugh.

'And what does *that* mean?'

Taking the time to explain it to him, Bay threw him a smile. 'Don't worry about it; I don't suppose I knew who he was at your age either. Got everything?'

'Certainly have!'

Slowing the car, Bay pulled off on to a side-road, and when they'd bumped along the dusty track for about a mile he pulled up outside a small white farmhouse. 'Be good; I'll see you in a couple of days.' Reaching for the book, he handed it to him. 'Don't forget this.'

'Hell no; Mary would go bananas. Have you signed it?'

'Of course.'

With a little grin, he shoved it into his bag. 'OK. Bye, Tug.'

Totally nonplussed, Jenna automatically took the map Mark handed her before he scrambled free and dashed off towards the front door.

Bay waited until it opened, was waved at by a dark-haired young woman, then turned the car and bumped back to the main road.

'He's not coming with us?' she asked stupidly.

'No, he's staying with English friends for a few days,' he murmured absently. 'Mary and John Dunbar. Didn't I say?'

'No.'

He gave her an odd glance. No, not odd, probing. 'You have a problem with that?'

'No.' Well, she didn't—or she didn't think she did; she just felt a vague disquiet. 'But if he wasn't coming with us,' she asked, puzzled, 'why did he invite me?'

Bay's bland smile made her want to hit him. Her voice slightly gritted, she asked, 'How much further is it?'

'Not far,' he murmured, and then he slowed, frowned, and pulled over to the side of the road.

Disquiet suddenly blooming to mammoth proportions, she asked worriedly, 'Is something wrong?'

'Wrong? No. Won't be a minute.' Taking the camera from her, he unlatched his door, climbed out and wandered off towards what looked like a ruined farmhouse.

Her eyes wide with astonishment and the residue of alarm, she stared after him, then blew her breath out in exasperation. Now what? Wait, she supposed. He'd presumably had an *idea*! And no doubt the real reason he'd invited her along was so that she could mind the car while he researched whatever it was he was researching. Watching his progress across the dusty plain towards the dwelling, she wondered how many other people had been suckered as she'd been suckered. Quite a few, probably. Not sure if she was

amused, or cross, she finally gave a wry smile, because, after all, she only had herself to blame.

He disappeared inside, re-emerged a few minutes
later at the rear, and then just stood and stared into
the distance. This sort of thing happened quite often,
she supposed, if you were a writer. And one just had
to hope, presumably, that he didn't wander off and
forget all about her while she sat obediently in the car
getting hotter and hotter. And her bad foot was
tingling. A horrible little niggle that usually presaged
a bout of pain. Great.

Thrusting open her door, gasping at the rush of
heat, she carefully stood. Closing the car door, leaning
back against it, she eased off her shoe. With luck, the
pain would be brief, although while it lasted it could
be terrifying in its ferocity. Gritting her teeth, she
waited, made a little whimper in the back of her
throat, clenched every muscle tight,

'*Now* you can drive,' Bay informed her quietly.

Snapping her head round, she stared at him. *Now*
is not a good time, she wanted to tell him. But if she
did she would have to explain, and she didn't want
to do that. 'Right,' she agreed, and she sounded hard,
she knew, because when the pain was bad she always
did. Pain caused tension and tension made her sound
terse. Easing her foot back into her shoe, her face
carefully averted, she limped round to the driver's
side. Thank God the car was an automatic, otherwise
she wouldn't have been able to manage. Equally
thankfully, his mind was on his research and not on
her. At least, she assumed that was what his mind was
on as he settled himself in the passenger seat and removed a pen and pad from the glove compartment.
Brows drawn into a frown, he began to write.

'Just follow this road, do I?'

'Mmm? Oh, yes.'

'And am I likely to be stranded in Albacete while you wander off again? No, don't answer that; I don't think I want to know.'

'Sorry?'

'Nothing,' she said shortly. She was aware that he glanced at her, probably speculatively, and she forced herself to smile. If she could just take a pain-killer, she thought, she'd be all right.

'You expected something different?' he asked quietly.

Puzzled, she glanced at him. 'Different? No.'

He was silent for a few moments, watching her, she knew, and then instructed, 'Take the next left. We'll have some lunch.'

Perhaps he thought eating was a cure for all ills. Certainly that was how it had sounded. Nodding to show she'd heard, she pulled over, drove along a narrow lane that allowed her a few fleeting glimpses of the small town in the distance, and into the courtyard of a *parador*. White walls dazzled the eye, a riot of colour from the gardens, tubs and hanging baskets delighted the senses, and, eager to unstick herself from the hot upholstery, stretch her bad leg, take a pain-killer, Jenna swung open her door the minute they stopped.

Her haste was her undoing. She stood too quickly, put her weight unthinkingly on her left leg—and gravity took care of the rest. Her knees took the brunt of her fall on to the raked gravel, but because she was on a slight incline, and despite flinging out her hands to save herself, almost in slow motion she continued forward on to her nose, slid a few inches along the stony ground and came to a halt.

Bay was still climbing out when she fell, and by the time he reached her she was already scrambling to her feet.

'I'm all right,' she insisted quickly. 'Don't fuss!'

'I never fuss,' he denied absently as he stared down into her poor grazed face, into eyes that glared their defiance.

'And don't laugh,' she choked.

'Why in God's name would I laugh?' he demanded. Reaching out as if to touch her, he changed his mind and pulled her gently into his arms instead, held her in a comforting embrace. Impersonal, but comforting. 'Poor sweetheart. I was too far away,' he murmured into her hair as though he were personally responsible.

'I know.' Her body became stiff as she tried to cope with this new pain, a sudden overwhelming feeling of wanting to stay where she was. She gritted her teeth, then jerked back to stare at him. 'How bad?' she demanded worriedly. Her nose felt as though it was broken at the very least.

He gave a compassionately rueful smile. 'Grazed. A bit bloody.'

'Oh, dear,' she said shakily.

'Knees?' He eased her further away and they both looked down. Blood was trickling down her left shin from beneath her white skirt. Bending, he eased the material higher, then sucked in his breath in sympathy at the sight of her torn and gritty knee. 'Oh, hell. Come on, let's get you inside and out of this sun.'

'Oh, no!' she exclaimed in horror. 'Not looking like this! Let me at least try to tidy myself a bit! Wipe the blood off!'

'Think they might refuse to let you in? They won't.' Not giving her another chance to argue, he put one arm round her waist, pushed the car door closed with his foot, and helped her towards the steps that led up to the foyer.

Well, at least she now had an excuse to limp, she thought, trying to make light of it, and, oddly enough, the pain in her nose and her knee seemed to have cancelled out the pain in her foot. Shock, she supposed, but she would have much preferred to tidy herself up a bit, examine her poor face before letting anyone else see her. And Bay might be laconic, give the impression he didn't know his left hand from his elbow, but he commanded instant attention and respect the moment he pushed through the heavy door and into the reception area. The clerk on duty gave a horrified cry and rushed round to assist. Jenna was helped into the manager's office, eased into a chair, orders were hastily issued, and within minutes a bowl of water, a towel and a small hand-mirror were brought, and feeling even more of a fool, she reluctantly accepted everyone's ministrations.

Bay, speaking in fluent Spanish—why was she surprised?—presumably explained the situation, directed operations, then knelt in front of her and began to bathe her knee carefully. Stiff with the anticipation that his touch would start off the pain in her foot that she didn't think she would ever learn to cope with, she stared fixedly at his bent head—and became aware instead of the almost erotic touch of his warm fingers on her skin. How very absurd.

The first-aid box was opened, distracting her, plasters found, and carefully applied. There were a few strands of grey in his thick dark hair, she noticed inconsequentially, and she had the absurd desire to reach out, thread her fingers through the tousled strands, grip them hard. Acutely aware of where her thoughts were taking her, she blushed faintly and quickly picked up the hand-mirror. She must have been more shaken up than she'd thought.

Almost afraid to look, afraid of what she would see, she stared reluctantly at her reflection. The skin on the bridge of her nose was torn, it looked as though grit had got into the cut, and blood was oozing in an intricate pattern towards her top lip. There was a small graze above her right eye and a dirty smudge on her chin. Charming. With a helpless shrug—because really, apart from looking a fright, it wasn't that ba 1, and apart from bathing it there was not very much she could do to mend matters—she put down the mirror, and gave Bay a wry smile that was shakier than she would have liked.

'I don't think it will scar,' he said quietly as he stood to continue his ministrations on her face.

'What? Oh, no, I don't suppose it will.' Not that it mattered, although judging by the flicker of surprise in his eyes she assumed that he thought it would. About to tell him that she really wasn't that vain, she hissed, then tried to relax as he dabbed carefully at her nose. Wiping away the blood, he stepped back to survey her.

'Hands?'

Glancing at them, then showing him, she insisted, 'They're fine. If I could just wash them.' She hated fuss, to be the centre of this sort of attention, and prayed that he would leave it there. Beyond giving her a rather searching glance, he did. And, knowing that if she didn't take a pain-killer soon she'd be climbing the walls, she asked shakily, 'Would you ask if there's a ladies' room I can use?'

He nodded, explained where it was, asked if she needed an escort, then luckily allowed her to escape.

Hands shaking, she wrenched off the top of the pill bottle, quickly swallowed one, then leaned on the white basin and stared at herself in the large mirror. She looked worse than she had after the coach accident. 'Oh, Jenna, Jenna,' she scolded herself softly as she began to wash her grazed hands carefully, 'you do get yourself in some pickles.' Carefully drying her hands, she gave a long sigh, and perched on a small stool to wait for the tablets to work.

When she returned to the reception area there was no sign of Bay, just a coarse-featured man. He watched her limp towards him, then gave a slow, leering, smile.

'All alone and in trouble, sweetheart?'

'No,' she denied distantly, 'merely waiting.'

'Well, I wouldn't leave a little darling like——' He broke off, and stared rather disconcertingly at Bay who had come silently to stand beside him. Jenna also glanced at him, and there was absolutely no trace of amiability about him now. He looked hard, and ever so slightly dangerous. The man obviously thought so too. He muttered something inarticulate and hurried across to the desk.

'I'm sorry,' Bay apologised quietly.

'Not your fault...'

'Entirely my fault,' he argued softly. 'Ready? I've arranged for the use of a room, and you can either have a meal sent up or coffee and sandwiches. Ready?'

'Yes, thank you, I'm very grateful, and coffee and sandwiches would be fine.' And she was grateful. Very. With his hand beneath her arm, they were shown up to the first floor by the porter. The warm brown tiled floors were polished until they shone, the white walls were hung with paintings and typically Spanish arte-facts, and everything was spotless. The room was spacious, with twin beds, an armchair, and *en-suite* bathroom.

The manager caught them up as Bay ushered her inside and sat her in the comfortable armchair in the corner; he was carrying a tray holding a glass of brandy. 'For shock,' Bay explained, 'and no need to look so embarrassed; we all do daft things from time to time.' Thanking the manager, and ordering sand-wiches and coffee for Jenna, he closed the door, glanced round to make sure she had everything, then perched on the edge of the bed nearest her.

Beginning to feel less shaky, the pain in her leg muted, and grateful to Bay for easing a difficult situ-ation, for calmly and competently dealing with every-thing without fuss or bother, she thanked him quietly.

'Nothing to thank me for,' he denied. 'Although it was indeed fortunate you didn't injure the hand that operates the camera,' he added with a dry smile. 'Then we would have been in the soup.'

'Oh, you wretch!' she exclaimed with a shaky laugh.

Comically raising and lowering his eyebrows, he got up to open the balcony doors, then stood for a moment staring out—as she stared at him. What sort of man was he? she wondered, not for the first time.

With so very little to latch on to, she had no idea what he thought, felt, wanted . . .

'Look,' she began awkwardly, 'if you need to go out and do more research or something, don't worry about me, I'll be fine.'

Turning his head, he smiled. 'Sure?'

'Yes, of course.'

He nodded. 'Your meal should be here soon, then have a warm bath, forty winks on the bed, while I investigate our surroundings, make notes, et cetera. Then, when I return, if you're feeling up to it, we'll go back to the complex. If you need anything else, just ring down to Reception.'

'I will, thanks, and I'm sorry for being such a pest.'

'I forgive you.' Quickly, adjusting the air-conditioning for her, he smiled and left. She heard his footsteps on the tiles of the corridor, heard him speak to someone, heard his quick laugh, then silence. Peace, or abandonment? She kept getting the feeling that she wanted to shake him, see what emerged—something *definite*, even if it was only a burst of temper. Surely no one could be so very controlled—not for real?

When the coffee and sandwiches arrived a few minutes later, her mind still on Bay, Jenna settled herself on the balcony and stared out over the grounds. There was a breeze here, and she tilted her face to it, allowed it to cool her hot cheeks. It was so quiet, she could almost believe she was the only person there, until a jet from a nearby airfield screamed noisily into the sky, frightening the life out of her. A military base perhaps; certainly that hurtling projectile would not have been carrying passengers. With a slight smile, she turned her attention to the grounds.

There was a tennis-court below her and, craning her neck to look round the corner, she saw the edge of what looked to be a swimming-pool.

Finishing her meal, and deciding to take Bay's advice, holding her skirt above her poor knee, she limped back inside.

The bath helped to ease the stiffness from her knee and, wrapping a large towel around herself, she applied a fresh plaster, blow-dried her hair with the drier provided, then lay thankfully on the bed. Not to sleep, she assured herself, but to drift pleasantly, try to forget her injuries. Her knee ached, and her nose throbbed, but mostly she just felt idiotic. What a way to shine in front of a man you fancied... No, more than fancied—liked very, very much. But she must not allow it to develop into more than that. Even if he'd been ordinary, which he clearly wasn't, she wasn't ready for another relationship—and knew that for the lie it was.

Sweetheart. He'd called her sweetheart. Not an endearment exactly, said only without thought to convey concern. Yet it had made her feel warm, special. Odd, that. Other men had used that same word, David included, and yet it had meant nothing. A likeable man. A very attractive, likeable man—or he gave a very good facsimile of one. And if he did, why? Why the need, or desire, to keep feelings hidden? Yet she wasn't wrong about the core of steel. She *knew* she wasn't, and thought that she wouldn't like to cross him. She had the feeling that he could be quite ruthless if the occasion demanded it; merciless. Not really very much like herself. Jenna was a believer in people—not always wise, of course, but she was ever the eternal optimist, and refused to become cynical about the letdowns. Naïve maybe, but it was hard to change a nature that was without guile. Open and friendly, she assumed others to be the same, and was often hurt when people lied or were malicious.

She woke suddenly, not knowing where she was. The room was dark, shadowy, the heavy shutters at the window pulled close. Oh, good grief, she hadn't meant to *sleep*. What on earth was the time? Switching on the bedside light, she groped for her watch—and saw Bay sitting in the armchair, watching her.

Her heart dipping alarmingly, she said stupidly, 'I didn't mean to sleep. You should have woken me.'

'For what purpose?' he asked lazily, and there was a disturbing note in his voice that made her go hot, then cold. Suddenly recalling that she was wearing nothing but a bath-sheet, she glanced hastily down to make sure she was decent, then gave a little sigh of relief. Flicking her eyes back to his, seeing the same disturbing quality, she tried to defuse it by giving a lame smile. He'd obviously showered, because his hair was damp, and that bothered her, because it meant he'd been here, wandering around, while she slept.

'I've taken the room next door,' he informed her laconically.

'Oh.' And what did that mean? That he'd showered in his own room, not hers? Or—something else?

'Not in any rush to get back to the complex, are you?'

'No,' she said cautiously.

'Then I thought we could have a decent meal here and stay the night.'

'Stay the night?' she repeated weakly. 'Here? But I don't even have a toothbrush!'

'The hotel will provide one.'

'But what about clean clothes? Underwear?'

'Wash your underwear out before you go to bed. It will soon dry,' he argued almost dismissively. Rising to his feet, his eyes still on hers, an expression in his eyes she didn't in the least understand, he stretched, arms high above his head, fingers linked, and she was aware of the play of muscles in his torso, of his flat stomach, hard thighs... Jenna! Stop it! 'I'll leave you to get dressed.' With a faint smile, he wandered out, closing the door softly behind him.

Stay the night, she repeated to herself. Separately. Yes, of course separately, she assured herself hastily. And don't keep *thinking* about it! Quickly dressing, rummaging in her handbag for lipstick and mascara, she stared critically at herself in the long mirror. A bit crumpled, but nothing much she could do about it, and, unless she sported a yashmak, her nose would have to remain in full view. Not a pretty sight. Oh, well, it would no doubt provide a talking point, and perhaps it would teach her to look where she was putting her feet in future. Not at all understanding why she felt so nervous, she walked out into the corridor and found Bay waiting patiently. He looked clean, vitally attractive, and she felt again that funny little flutter along her nerves.

He stared at her for a moment, holding her eyes just for a second, then he smiled. Jenna was quite unaware that her sore nose, far from detracting from her beauty, merely added an element of fragility. Being quite without conceit, she was more often than not embarrassed rather than grateful at the many compliments she received.

'Ready?'

'Yes, of course.'

He nodded, took her elbow, and escorted her down to the restaurant.

The meal was excellent, the service superior. Nothing seemed too much trouble, and when Jenna reluctantly confessed quietly to Bay that she wasn't very hungry, that she didn't think she could manage all three courses, the head waiter's opinion was quietly sought. He smiled understandingly at Jenna, assured her, in impeccable English, that of course she was not being a nuisance, and went to confer with the chef. No one else in the dining-room suffered, was made to wait, or was probably even aware of the small departure from the norm going on at their table. They weren't being given preferential treatment although maybe they were, just a little bit, she thought with an inward smile, because she guessed that Bay, without the least effort on his part, automatically received the sort of service that most people yearned for.

Meanwhile, his appearance, his manner, his quiet competence, were slowly and insidiously undermining her determination not to become emotionally involved. He was the sort of escort every girl yearned for and so seldom found. Interesting, at ease, comfortable with his own masculinity, and with the knack of making a woman feel special.

He listened to her as though what she said was of the utmost importance. There were no awkward silences, no sexual innuendoes, no over-the-top compliments. For her part, Jenna wanted to know what went on inside his head; wanted to know about his life; what he was really like. Why there was that faint, elusive barrier between himself and the world, as though he always held himself apart. A barrier that was intriguing.

When the waiter returned, it was with a suggestion
of a light soup, a small piece of white fish with some
fresh vegetables, one glass of wine, and an early night.
Jenna wondered if the owners of the *parador* knew
what an asset they had, not only in their choice of
head waiter, but in their manager. What a difference
it made when people were kind and friendly. And she
wondered if Bay knew the effect he had on people,
not only women—on this woman in particular.
Probably. But he thought her a butterfly. An experienced butterfly, she suspected, which was perhaps just
as well—emotional involvement with this man would
be stupid. She thought he probably had the ability to
hurt her, and more pain she did not need right now.

When she had eaten most of what had been put
before her, still feeling unbelievably tired, emotionally
and physically battered, she quietly excused herself.
It was wretched, she thought, to be with a man like
this and not be able to be yourself, but probably all
for the best.

'No, no,' she denied as Bay would have risen, 'you
stay and finish your meal. I'll be fine. Honestly.'

Ignoring her protest, indicating to their waiter that
he would be back, he escorted Jenna from the dining
area, and up to her room. 'It's quite thoroughly
shaken you up, hasn't it?' he asked gently as he opened
her door for her.

'Yes,' she agreed, with a little moue of disgust for
her behaviour. Far more, in fact, than it should have
done, would probably normally have done, but
coming so close after the other accident, the fact that
a good night's sleep was something of a rarity, her
system was obviously still a bit unsettled. 'I'm be-

having like an invalid, and I do so *hate* people who do that. I am sorry to have spoiled your evening.'

'You haven't spoiled it in the least. Get a good night's sleep. I'll see you in the morning.' He nodded, gave a half-smile that was no sort of smile at all, and walked away.

Conscious of disappointment, and a feeling of let-down, she went to get ready for bed. Washing out her underwear, she hung it over the towel-rail to dry. Then the absurdity of it all overcame her, and she grinned. She'd come to Spain to recover from an accident, had been filled with eager anticipation of seeing all the sights, and, so far, had seen the outside of a few buildings in Madrid, a great deal of countryside, and now, due to *another* accident, the inside of a *parador*! She just hoped no one asked her what Albacete was like, because she would be hard put to it to tell them! She might have done better to have stayed at home. But then she would not have met Bay. Bay, who was laconic—and wary. The thought suddenly popped into her head. But it was true, she realised. She'd been puzzling all day over that odd expression in his eyes. It wasn't only cynical amusement; there had been wariness there too. Why? she wondered. What had he to be wary of?

Lying on the bed, partly because of the heat, partly because lying inside the covers would have rubbed her injured leg, and trying to keep her head still on the pillow, not burrow it as she usually did, she continued to wonder about it. She tried to consider Bay's odd behaviour dispassionately, but tiredness overcame her and she slept.

It was not perhaps surprising after the fall in the car park that she had one of her nightmares. As her

sleep deepened, she began moaning softly, turning this
way and that on the rumpled bed, as she tried to
escape from the twisted metal of a coach that was
hurtling down an incline far steeper than the original
reality. And in the dream her metal prison was
smaller—a tin coffin that crushed her ribs, her legs—
and there were no rescuers, no friendly firemen with
cutting equipment, only the cold metal that continued to crush her with malevolent ease. Alone, and
trapped, her cries for help unheard, she gave a last
gasping cry, and snapped awake. Heart racing, she
stared into the shadowy room, and only slowly let her
breath out on a long, shuddery sigh. A dream, just a
dream, but her leg was throbbing, her foot cramped.
With a despairing little groan, she swung her legs
carefully off the side of the bed and sat up.

'Damn you,' she cried softly, 'can't you let me get
at least one good night's sleep?' Obviously not.
Getting to her feet, she snapped on the bedside light.
Hobbling in search of her bag, and the pain-killers it
contained, she halted halfway across the floor, and
frowned. She *always* knew where her bag was. *Always*,
because it contained her money, credit cards, passport,
and she was always very careful of its safety. So where
was it? She'd had it in the restaurant...

Oh, no. Oh, Jenna, you idiot.

Glancing at the bedside clock, she saw that it was
gone three. The restaurant would be long closed. So
where would they have put it if they'd found it? In
the manager's safe? Or Bay, she suddenly wondered.
Had it been handed to him? She couldn't leave it;
apart from her valuables, it contained the pain-killers,
and those she *had* to have.

Teeth gritted on the pain, she shrugged into the white towelling robe left in the bathroom for guests, cautiously opened her door, and peered out on to the dark landing. Feeling like a fool, she tapped hesitantly on Bay's door, then put her ear against it to listen. Nothing. And if she banged harder she might wake everyone else on this floor. Balcony, she suddenly remembered. Next door's balcony adjoined hers, just a low railing to separate them. If his shutters were open . . .

Hobbling back, quietly closing her door, she went out through the French doors and peered across at Bay's room. His windows were also open; she could see the filmy nets blowing gently. Best to look there first before going down to Reception and trying to persuade the night manager to look for it. She might even be able to see it, not even have to wake Bay up.

Stepping carefully over the dividing railing, bottom lip clenched between her teeth as she tried to make no sound, she peered into his room. Giving herself a second for her eyes to accustom themselves to the dark, she slowly quartered the room, trying to identify individual objects, and to keep her eyes firmly averted from the hump on the bed that was Bay.

There was a large, dark object on the bedside table; it *could* be her bag—it was the right shape. Careful not to trip over anything, stub her toe, she limped towards it, reached out—and with whiplash speed her wrist was captured and she was dragged down on to the bed.

CHAPTER FOUR

JENNA'S scream of alarm was cut off by a large, warm palm. 'I wondered how long it would take,' Bay murmured softly, his voice a mere breath of sound, and before she could react, answer, explain, his hand had been replaced by his mouth.

Shocked, almost stunned, after her first little jerk of reaction, she lay still, as though powerless to move. His mouth was warm, dry, and incredibly gentle, which was perhaps why she didn't immediately see it as a threat. She parted her mouth, to protest, she thought, but he obviously took it as invitation, because the kiss deepened. His hand slid beneath her neck, beneath her hair! and careful of her sore nose, he teased her lips further apart, touched his tongue fleetingly to hers.

She could feel the tension in him, the careful way he was holding himself, and a flood of emotion swept through her, made her raise her arms, hold him loosely, then tighter, and when he gave a little groan in the back of his throat it was she, not he who moved closer. She could feel the heat of his naked flesh, the warmth of his loins, and his bare feet began to rub against hers. The right, she thought hazily; if it had been the left...

She was only covered by a flimsy bathrobe, no protection at all as his warm palm smoothed up over her ribcage, came to rest below her breast. All she could think was that she hadn't felt like this with David;

had never felt like this with anyone—so hot, so wanting, so—afraid. Not of him, of what he might do, but of herself, the feelings that seemed to be swamping her.

He was kissing her as though it was a compulsion, and she could so easily feel his arousal against her, wanted more than anything in the world to shrug her robe aside, touch her flesh to his—and that was so silly, because she barely knew him, and she didn't behave like this, ever. She didn't think she would ever have believed that choices were so hard to make—so hard not to give in to what her body was telling her to do.

He released her mouth, and she slowly opened her eyes, stared up at him. Feeling almost numb, incapable of movement, she was aware with only half her attention that she was practically naked, that the robe had come undone, exposing her breasts, one leg, and she could still feel the warmth, the hardness of his foot, the involuntary flexing of his toes. Moving her hand, about to touch it to his face, she stilled. You didn't touch your fingers to coal that was still hot.

'That what you wanted?' he asked quietly, and it took her a moment to comprehend the derision.

'What?' she asked weakly.

Rolling to the side, he snapped on the small bedside light, linked his hands behind his head, and stared up at the ceiling. 'Fame doesn't rub off, you know.'

'What?'

'And if I'd wanted you in my bed,' he drawled even more quietly, 'I would have invited you.'

Jerking upright, she stared at him, a deep frown in her eyes. '*What?*'

He turned his head towards her, raising one eyebrow.

Still staring at him, comprehension slow to dawn, she denied furiously. 'I didn't *want* to be invited!'

'Did you not?'

'No!'

'Then why, pray, were you groping around my room?'

'I was looking for my bag!'

'In the middle of the night?' he asked sceptically.

'Yes! And are you accusing me of...? And what do you mean, fame doesn't rub off? You think I came because you're *famous*? I didn't ask for this! You grabbed *me*, kissed me... as though you *meant* it!'

'Illusion,' he scoffed. 'Acting, if you like, at which a writer—a good writer—is usually very skilled.' With a slow smile, a very nasty sort of smile that shocked her, he removed one hand from beneath his neck and slowly trailed it between her breasts.

Slapping his hand away, dragging her robe closed, she demanded angrily, 'You really think I came for this?'

'Of course I do.'

'Then that makes you incredibly stupid!'

'I'm never stupid,' he denied mockingly, 'and very rarely wrong. Admittedly, for a while today I wondered if I'd been mistaken... But so nice to be proved right.' Pushing her flat, he rolled to cover her, and as his naked thigh touched hers she dragged her breath into her lungs with a quick jerk, then went rigid when his hand grasped her chin, held her head steady, before he kissed her, very hard, very thoroughly, very—expertly.

With a little shudder, she tried to push him away.
He refused to be pushed.

'I know that you wondered why I had allowed Mark
to invite you,' he said softly, his face barely inches
from hers, 'but it wasn't for this. It was for no better
reason than I thought I should enjoy your company.
Not your *intimate* company,' he emphasised, 'just
your company.'

'And you thought I knew the rules,' she stated
pithily—shakily, but pithily. And never, she thought,
had she been more aware of a man's naked flesh than
she was right now. Warm, naked flesh, firm, one thigh
resting between hers . . . 'Get off me!' she gritted.

'Too late to protest, Jenna,' he drawled softly. 'Far,
far too late. You left your bag——'

'By *accident*!'

'Which as an excuse, I have to admit, was
excellent . . .'

'Will you stop it? I came for my bag—*only* my bag!
Certainly not for a lesson in——'

'Arousal?'

'I don't *need* lessons,' she snarled furiously.

'No,' he conceded on a long drawl. 'So I suspected—and subsequently discovered.'

'Ohh . . .' Teeth gritted, she shoved him to one side,
wrenched her robe out from under him, and, embar-
rassingly aware that she was showing far more than
she was covering, she levered herself across his inert,
and very naked body, and scrambled free. 'You have
to be the most . . .' Chest heaving with temper, unable
to think of *anything* to say that would squash his
enormous conceit, she snatched up her bag.

'If you didn't want it,' he mused softly, 'I wonder
why you didn't try very hard to escape?'

Because of my leg! she wanted to shout. Because I
was afraid that struggling would *hurt* it! Only that
wasn't very truthful, she thought furiously as she
limped towards the French doors—she hadn't
struggled because she had thought he *meant* it! And
because it was what she wanted. 'I came for my bag,'
she repeated stonily, more in justification for herself
than for him.

'Then tell me why you wanted it at three in the
morning and, if I was wrong, I'll apologise.'

Swinging round on him, one hand holding the door-
frame for balance, thankful to see that he'd at least
draped the sheet across his nakedness, she denied
angrily, 'I don't *want* your apology. I don't want *anything* from you! I wanted my bag because it contains
something I *need*!'

Not waiting for an answer, she limped across the
balcony and into her room. And why, *why*, she demanded of herself as she limped into the bathroom
to take a pain-killer, did everyone always have to turn
out less than she had thought them? It had been fun,
and nice—a little light flirtation, a distraction...
Mouth tight, she wrenched the top off the bottle,
shook two tablets into her hand and defiantly
swallowed them. She hadn't wanted involvement,
commitment—just a nice time! And how *dared* he
think she'd gone into his room for sex? She wasn't
like that! Just because she'd worn a skimpy black
swimsuit, flirted with him... And he must be a
damned good actor if he could simulate *arousal*!

Leaning her face against the cool tiles, she sighed,
waited for the pain-killers to work, and then limped
slowly back to bed. Why did people have to be so
wrong? And now there was a little lump in her throat

and an ache in her chest which had nothing whatever
to do with the pain in her leg or the aftermath of her
nightmare. But if that was what he thought of her,
then that was what she would allow him to think. *She*
knew she had only gone to collect her bag.

It was a long time before she got back to sleep, and
when she woke in the morning to a sharp knock on
her door she felt—depressed. Something else to be
hidden.

Surprised, but grateful, when she discovered that
breakfast was being delivered to her, she smiled,
thanked the waiter, and forced herself to eat two warm
croissants and drink a cup of coffee. Reluctant to face
Bay, but knowing there was no choice, she washed,
dressed, and was sitting waiting when he came for
her—and not by a word or a glance would she ever
let him know how he had hurt or misjudged her.

'I'm all ready,' she informed him with quiet dignity,
and, picking up her bag, slinging it over her shoulder,
she accompanied him downstairs. Returning her key
to Reception, she smiled, thanked them, and walked
ahead of Bay out to the car.

Before starting the engine, he glanced at her, pursed
his lips slightly, and began quietly, '*If* I was wrong...'

Taking in a small breath, she turned to face him,
her expression neutral. 'You *were* wrong, but it happened, and whatever interpretation you put on it no
longer matters. Some you win, some you lose,' she
added flippantly, and let him take *that* how he chose.

'Then why did you agree to come on the trip?'

'Because I thought it would be enjoyable, a chance
to see some of the countryside—*not* because I wanted
your body! And if you thought *that* of me, why allow
Mark to invite me? Why in fact *did* he invite me if

he wasn't even going to be here? Because I was kind to him?'

'In my experience, people are very rarely kind for kindness's sake.'

'Then you've been meeting all the wrong people!'

'Possibly.'

Face tight, she demanded, 'You think it was a *ploy*? Which presupposes that I actually knew who Mark was, which you know very well I didn't. And, even if I had, it's hardly flattering to your brother.'

'No, although it happens. But I believe Mark invited you because he thought you would be a suitable companion for me,' he drawled. 'No threat, you understand. He seems to be of the opinion that you are gentle and sweet.'

'How intuitive of him,' she said with saccharine fury.

'And I suspect, to put Clarissa's nose out of joint.'

'Then let's hope it worked! Can we go now?'

He nodded, switched on the engine.

'And if this is what being famous means—being suspicious of everyone and everything—then I am very glad I'm *ordinary*!'

'Ordinary?' he scoffed with a hollow laugh. 'Oh, no, Jenna, you aren't ordinary.'

'Ah, yes,' she agreed pithily, 'I forgot. What was it you called me—a sensualist? And sensualists are never ordinary, are they? They go into men's rooms in the middle of the night——' Breaking off, she gave a sigh of disgust, and turned round to stare out of the window. And what had she thought about underlying steel? Well, add *blinkered*! 'And for a writer,' she muttered under her breath, 'you seem to be sadly lacking in intuition!'

He didn't answer. Not that she had expected him to, but after that, apart from him asking if she wanted to stop for a coffee, the trip back was accomplished in silence. Not a comfortable silence—his the silence of indifference, presumably, hers of fury and bitter disappointment.

When he pulled up outside her villa, he merely waited, didn't switch off the engine.

'Thank you for the trip,' she said, punctiliously polite. 'I can honestly say it was educational!'

'Good. I hope your injuries soon heal.'

'Thank you.' Climbing out, she walked carefully up to her door, fought not to limp, until she heard his car pull away, then her shoulders slumped tiredly. Feeling unutterably exhausted, she went inside. And what sort of life had he had to make him so damned suspicious? Best forget him, Jenna, she told herself. Yes. Only she didn't think it would be that easy.

The next few days settled into a pattern; she spent the mornings sightseeing and the afternoons by her pool. The first time Mark dropped by, she gave him her friendly smile.

'Hi. Have a good time with your friends?'

'Yeah, it was neat. Haven't seen the AP have you?'

'No,' she said quietly, nor was she likely to, but no need to tell Mark that.

'Oh. Oh, well, I expect I'll find him.' He hovered for a few moments longer, gave her a curiously sweet smile, and then wandered off. He made further brief appearances in her garden over the next two days. His brother didn't. Because he was writing? Or because he was avoiding her? She hoped that the long walk round the roadway which he was presumably having to make was irritating him. Her leg also seemed to have become more painful—because she had been doing too much probably. A scab was beginning to form on her knee, and her nose—hardly attractive—but for the most part she forgot all about them. It was her calf and her foot which were causing the trouble—and her thoughts. Sleepless nights were also beginning to take their toll, and when she emerged rather later than usual the following morning, dark shadows beneath her lovely eyes, she was in no mood to face the rather drab-looking young woman with horn-rimmed glasses who was hovering on her lawn.

'Oh, hi,' she gushed, with a rather embarrassed smile. 'I was looking for Bay. You haven't seen him, have you?'

'No, sorry,' Jenna replied.

Pulling a face that was a sort of cross between worried and timid, she muttered, 'He really is naughty. He knew I wanted to talk to him this morning—not that I expect him to drop what he's doing just because *I* want him to, you understand, but he does tend, when he's bored, or having trouble with a plot, to just wander off. I find him talking to the most extra-ordinary people, you know. Or flirting with all the pretty girls—and then he looks totally astonished and blames me when they all turn up on his doorstep!'

Idly wondering which category she came into, extraordinary or pretty, and wondering if she ought to explain that there was no danger of *her* turning up on his doorstep, she asked, 'Are you by any chance Clarissa?'

'Why, yes. Sorry, I thought you knew.'

'No; how would I know?' Mark had given the impression that she was bossy and authoritative, which was not at all the impression that this girl gave. In fact, she looked as though one harsh word would have her in tears.

'Hmm?' With an abstracted air, winding one piece of hair round and round her finger, she looked around her, almost as though expecting Bay to appear like the genie from the lamp. 'I wonder if he went down to the shops? Perhaps I should go and look there. He isn't golfing, because there's a competition on today.'

Not entirely sure what sort of response was expected of her, Jenna just continued to stand there.

With a bright, social smile, her frown banished, Clarissa turned back to Jenna. 'Oh, well, not to worry; I expect I'll find him. Did you like Albacete?' she suddenly asked.

'Oh, yes, thank you. It was fine.'

'Good. Bay said he'd given you a little treat.'

Treat? 'Did he?' And had being dragged into his bed been part of it?

'Yes. He does that sometimes. Different people give him different ideas, I think. Although I am surprised, because you're like Maureen. At least, he said you were.'

'Maureen?'

'Yes. The same sort of, well, *clever* look.'

'Clever,' Jenna repeated. 'I see. And who is Maureen?' Not that she was really interested, she assured herself.

'Who?'

'Yes, who.'

'Oh.' With a return to her worried air—Jenna couldn't quite decide whether it was manufactured or not—she bit her lip. 'Sorry; I thought you probably knew. My own fault, of course, jumping to conclusions, which I *shouldn't* do, being in a position of trust and everything. I am his research assistant, after all,' she added, presumably just in case Jenna didn't know.

'Yes.' She made it sound as though it were on a par with being handmaiden to the Queen. Don't be bitchy, Jenna, she told herself.

'Well, I must get on; so sorry if I've been a nuisance, but if you do see him would you kindly tell him that I'm looking for him?'

'Yes, of course.'

'Oh, and—er—best not to say that I mentioned Maureen. He might not want you to know.' With a vague smile, she wandered round the side of the villa and squeezed herself between the walls.

So that was Clarissa. Jenna could quite see why she would exasperate Mark. It was very difficult to counteract half-statements and innuendo. Also difficult to know if her nose had been put out of joint.

Settling herself on her lounger, she stared up at the blue sky. So he got bored, did he, and then went off to flirt with pretty girls? And he'd given her a treat. Wow.

And because she wasn't paying very much attention to anything, because her mind was centred on what Clarissa had said, because she was feeling hurt and extremely disillusioned, she didn't hear him approach. One minute she was alone, the next he was standing beside her. With a little start, she turned her head—and her heart lurched. He was bare-chested, with an old pair of jeans clinging snugly to his narrow hips, but there was no amusement lurking in his eyes or around his mouth. Neither could she persuade herself that he was still tense, as he had been on the drive back from Albacete. She was: her muscles had involuntarily cramped when he'd appeared. But whatever tension he had evinced before it was no longer in evidence. He'd obviously got over whatever it had been.

'How are you?'

'Fine. Any reason I shouldn't be?'

He shrugged, gave her a rather searching look. 'You're late up today.'

'Am I?' And how did he know?

'Mmm. Not feeling too good? You look tired.'

'No, I'm fine,' she lied. 'Too many late nights, I expect. The dreaded Clarissa was just here,' she mentioned quickly in order to change the subject. 'She said she was looking for you.'

'Yes, I've just seen her, and she's not so dreaded. She's off to Cartagena to do some research.'

Ah, so that was how he knew she was late up. She wondered how Clarissa might have phrased it. So sorry to tell you, but Jenna was late up today. 'And now you're at a loose end?' she queried harshly. 'Or got fed up using the long way round?'

He looked puzzled for a moment, then understanding. 'Ah. Make my peace to save my legs? No, I merely came to see how you were. Mark mentioned that you looked tired.'

'Did he? Who's Maureen?' she asked bluntly. This Maureen that no one must mention. Someone he'd had an affair with? Someone like herself. Maureen, who was clever.

He narrowed his eyes, then gave her a bland look. 'No one who need worry you. I'll see you later, I expect.' With a languid wave of his hand, he moved away, disappearing using the same unorthodox method as previously.

Slumping tiredly, she lay down and tilted her hat over her face. It was best this way. Yes. But it didn't feel it. It felt wretched. And being normally friendly wouldn't have hurt anybody, would it? Yes, it would; it would have hurt herself. She could have explained, let him apologise—and then what? Nothing. Anyway, she'd be going home soon. Best not to get involved. And her leg hurt; and she wanted to grizzle. And if you don't want to become addicted to pain-killers, I suggest you stay put for a few days, she told herself almost savagely, and perfect your acting!

At least she'd managed to visit Los Belones, the nearest village, she comforted herself, and the Strip, the long piece of land that jutted out from Cabo de Palos. She'd driven up one way, then back the other, and didn't like it. She preferred the old Spain, not this new tourist attraction with its glitzy buildings, even one that looked like a pink wedding-cake, if you please. With absolutely no desire to linger, or even walk along parts of it, she'd idly watched the sail-boats on the Mar Menor, turned up her nose at bars with names like Harry's, and returned to the complex. And she refused to admit that all this activity had been because she thought it best to avoid Bay. Not that it had done her much good, because she only had to close her eyes to feel his warmth against her, his mouth touching hers, and that humiliation she'd felt when he'd accused her of seduction. And lying by the pool-side just to get brown seemed even more absurd. Hot, irritable, she flung off her hat and made her way to the pool.

When she went to ring her mother that evening, the phone wouldn't work—just one more irritation in a life that was becoming strewn with them. And if she didn't ring her mother would worry, automatically assume that her darling daughter had fallen down a hole or something. Accident-prone to the point of insanity, she knew exactly what her mother would think if she didn't get in touch. And because she loved her, didn't want her to worry, she would now have to make an *effort*.

She knew the complex had its own telephone exchange... She didn't know where it *was*, but she knew that they had one, so she either had to go looking for it, which meant getting the car out, or go next door to the mysterious Peter, whom she still hadn't met, and who Helen had assured her would be her constant guide and mentor. Mmm, so constant, she hadn't even seen him! Probably the poor chap hadn't wanted to be her guide and mentor and was sensibly keeping a low profile. Oh, well, nothing ventured, nothing gained, and Helen had assured her that he was there to be used in an emergency. And wasn't this an emergency? It was.

Forcing herself not to limp, just in case anyone was watching, she clambered awkwardly over the low dividing hedge, and rang the bell of the villa next door. Staring out over the distant hills, she waited, then rang again. Nothing. Oh, hell, and probably the reason she hadn't seen him was because he wasn't even here!

Limping backwards, she stared up at the front of the villa. An upstairs window was open, which meant—what? Chewing indecisively on her lower lip, she called tentatively, 'Peter?'

'Go away.' The voice issuing from the open window was familiar—very, very familiar. Her brows drew into a frown as she continued to stare upwards. Bay Rawson in Peter's villa meant—what? That his real

name was Peter? That Rawson was a *nom de plume*?
It would account for the fact, wouldn't it, that she
never saw Peter? Ah, but if he was Peter, why did he
keep coming through the hedge at the bottom of her
garden? Why not go through his own? Why not come
round the front? She had no idea, yet if he was Peter,
and it was indeed him that Helen had asked to keep
an eye on her, that would explain, wouldn't it, his
continuing presence in her life? Not because he liked
her, but because Helen had asked him to. In which
case... In which case, what? It might explain his in-
viting her to Albacete, but it didn't explain his behaviour at the *parador*! Or insulting her the next
morning! And suddenly deciding that she needed it
clarified, never mind the wretched phone, she called,
'*Are* you Peter?'

'Go away, Jenna. I'm busy.'

Writing? And on no account must be disturbed?
Well, she didn't *want* to disturb him, any more than
she had wanted him to disturb her; she just wanted
to use the phone. 'Look, I am sorry about this, but
could I——?'

'No.' He didn't sound angry, or impatient, just
abominably indifferent.

'But you don't know what I'm going to ask you!'

'The answer's still no. Don't you ever learn?' And
he reached out and shut the window.

CHAPTER FIVE

DON'T you ever learn...? He thought, he actually thought... With a sour smile of disgust, Jenna turned and limped awkwardly back to her own villa. She just hoped he needed to use *her* phone one day! Or anything else! Any favour at *all* in fact!

Angrily snatching up her car keys, she drove to the telephone exchange to report the fault.

She had no more visitors that day, which was probably just as well, the mood Peter, or Bay, or whatever his name was, had put her in.

The following morning as she assembled all her necessary bits and pieces on the terrace—her book, towel, sun-cream, hat—there were sounds of dissension from one of the other villas. It was hard to tell from which one exactly, but one of the voices definitely sounded like Mark. Was Clarissa back? Had psychology been abandoned? Trying to summon up some enthusiasm, or at least interest, expecting a visit at *any* moment, she tuned out and settled herself for a morning's sunbathing before the sun got too hot. Half an hour later, she had her first visitor. Not Mark, as she had expected, but his brother. She glanced at him, then quickly away, and if he thought she was going to demand an explanation for his behaviour the evening before he would be disappointed. If he thought she was going to *explain* he would be disappointed.

79

He came to stand beside her, stared at her for some moments in silence. 'You lost your bag again?'

With a bitter little laugh, she shook her head. Totally unsurprised by his flat tone, only surprised that she had ever been taken in by him, she replied equally flatly, 'No, *Peter*, I did not lose my bag. Neither did I want your body. I merely wished to use the phone. Why couldn't you have told me you were Peter, instead of playing all these silly games?'

'Why did you need to use the phone?'

'Because mine didn't work.'

'I see.'

'Good.'

There was speculation in his steady gaze as he stared down at her, and not wishing to give the impression that she actually *cared*, which of course she didn't, she assured herself, she abandoned her lofty tone, and gave him a sugary smile. 'Worry not, it is now fixed. Although, due to your odd behaviour, I was forced into activity,' she scolded reproachfully. 'I had to drive to the telephone exchange.'

'A marathon journey,' he agreed solemnly, 'fraught with untold dangers.'

'Exactly.'

'Then I will tender an apology, and my——'

'An apology is not needed,' she interrupted quickly. 'Apologies from you are *never* needed, although I dare say your visit has nothing to do with yesterday, but more because you're trying to avoid the motley collection of people in your own villa. I assume that is where the row was coming from earlier?'

He gave his slow smile, an extraordinarily derisive smile. 'You know me so well.'

'I don't know you at all! Including your name—or which villa you currently inhabit.' Would he have tendered an apology if her explanation hadn't been acceptable? Might it not have been better if it hadn't? No point in probing, and, because it was vitally important that he think her indifferent, she asked with absent curiosity, 'Why do you keep appearing through the hedge at the bottom of my garden?'

'Because it's easier to get through that way. If one is on foot, it saves a hard slog round the roadway.'

'I know that. I meant, if you live next door, why do you need to? Why does Mark need to?'

'My dear girl, I don't even *pretend* to understand the workings of a thirteen-year-old mind.'

She imagined he did. She imagined he understood a great many things he wasn't prepared to admit. And if he didn't want to answer, wanted secrets... With a pretended philosophical shrug, she murmured, 'Oh, well, and if Helen approves of all this activity, who am I to object?'

'I don't know. Do you object?'

'No,' she denied helplessly.

'Good. So who is Helen?'

With a comical return to her confusion she prompted, 'The woman who lent me this villa?'

'Ah.'

'You don't know her?'

'Sadly not.'

Frowning, she continued, 'But she said...'

'What did she say?' he asked helpfully when she came to a lame halt.

'Nothing,' she said quickly, because if he didn't know Helen, then obviously Helen couldn't have told him about her, in which case she most definitely wasn't going to either. Abruptly changing the subject, she tilted her head on one side and commented, 'You don't look like a Peter.'

'No,' he agreed amiably. 'Presumably my mother didn't think so either.'

Staring at him, and beginning to wonder just how many other inconsequential paths this wretched man was intending to lead her down, she asked, perplexed, 'She didn't?'

'No, but if you wish to call me Peter, then please feel free to do so,' he offered helpfully. 'I'm sure I could get used to it in time.'

Irritated, she queried, 'Peter isn't your real name?'

'No. Bayne is my real name.'

'Then what were you doing next door? Visiting Peter?'

Devilish amusement in his eyes, he shook his head. 'Peter had to trundle off to New York for some reason or another.'

'Then what on earth were you doing in his villa? Burgling the place?'

'Good heavens, no,' he denied reproachfully. 'I was attempting to gain some much needed peace and quiet in order to write.'

'In someone else's villa? When they are away?' she demanded in scandalised accents.

'Mmm. Peter doesn't mind—he's used to me popping in and out.'

'I see. So did *he* tell you about me?'

About to settle himself on the grass, he halted and stared at her quizzically for a moment, then gave his cynical smile. 'Now, what to answer? If I deny it, you might be offended, and if I admit it—what exactly is he supposed to have told me? It's a puzzle, isn't it?'

'Yes, but seeing as offending me is something you have down to a fine art,' she retorted waspishly, 'it's a little difficult to believe that one more offence is going to bother you.' With a sweet smile, fighting to remain immune, and gathering that Peter hadn't in fact told him anything, she relaxed again.

'You've chipped a nail,' he offered helpfully.

Glancing down, she gave a helpless nod. 'So I have. I'll see to it later.'

'Yes. Can't have the perfection marred, can we?'

'Certainly not,' she agreed.

'So what are you intending to do today?'

'Oh, today I thought I'd just laze around, go for a swim maybe. Just by way of a change.'

'As opposed to having a swim and then lazing around?'

'Mmm.'

'Wholly admirable,' he agreed. 'What time is it?'

Glancing at her watch, she murmured, 'Ten past twelve.'

'Is it? Oh, hell, how time does fly.' With a sketchy salute, he walked off.

Staring rather blankly after him, Jenna felt her eyes fill with tears. Bayne Rawson, author—fêted, chased, and lacking in intuition. No, that wasn't strictly fair; she was the one who'd allowed the farce to continue. If she tried to explain now, he wouldn't believe her. And she'd allowed her guard to drop again, hadn't she? And did he need the peace and quiet of Peter's villa because people kept appearing on his doorstep? Like pretty girls?

Feeling miserable and confused, not even liking herself very much, she settled back on to the lounger. Perhaps she should leave, take herself out of his orbit

before... Before what? Before they came to blows?
Why did it even *matter* what he thought of her? She
didn't know, only that it did. So why didn't she just
be herself—explain? And if he disliked her as much
as he said he did, why didn't he just ignore her? Why
keep dropping by?

Confused, irritable, she continued to brood about
him. And if he came back? Might be wise to take
herself off for the afternoon. She could drive into
Cartagena—or, as the Spanish pronounced it,
Cartahena—try to find a parking space near to the
ancient port, have a slow look round. And she wanted
his amused smiles again; wanted him to kiss her;
wanted to feel again the warmth of his arms around
her; wanted to know what it felt like to be liked by
him. Such a fool.

Red earth, new roads, the old and the modern jostled
side by side as she drove towards Cartagena. And La
Union, the first little community she drove through,
looked as though it might once have been a thriving
mining town. On the hillsides beyond it were what
looked like old mine workings, abandoned equipment.
Had the town once echoed to the shouts of miners
and the noise of machinery? Perhaps she could get a
book on it—or perhaps Bay would know.

She followed the main route through Cartagena,
hoping to get an overall impression of the ancient
town, trying to get a glimpse of the shops, find somewhere to park, and eventually wound up back at the
port, where she paid a small sum to a smiling young
man for the privilege of parking on some waste
ground. You had to admire enterprise!

Walking slowly along the road, she lingered to stare at a beached submarine highlighted by jets of water. To lend credence? she wondered in forced amusement. Yet nothing could disguise the fact that it was out of its element. A wartime relic with a once proud record? Deeds of daring do? Unfortunately, her Spanish wasn't good enough to enable her to read the inscription. Maybe Bay would know. And if you don't damned well stop relating everything to Bay, I will get very cross with you, Jenna! she told herself.

With a big sigh, she continued on her way. There was so much she wanted to see, explore, and tantalising glimpses down side-streets that she knew her leg would not allow her to walk down were hardly satisfying. Old buildings, mellowed with age; gardens. Perhaps it would have been better to stay at home, she thought, with a small despondent sigh, not come to new and exciting places that she was unable to do more than look fleetingly at. Curious by nature, she found it frustrating not to be able to wander where she willed, where her mind wanted to lead her.

Unfortunately, the cobbles along the alley she was tempted down were not very kind to her bad foot, and she was forced to stop and look into every shop she came to, pretend an absorption in fishing tackle, tins of soup, and then a bookshop, and bang went her determination to put Bay out of her mind. Emblazoned across the shop window, proclaiming that his new book was in stock, was his name. Obviously a great deal better known than she had expected, especially in a foreign country. But fame didn't rub off, did it? He'd said so.

Turning away, deliberately refusing to buy his book, she retraced her steps. Driving back, she saw a sign for the complex where she didn't expect to see a sign, and, her curiosity getting the better of her, she drove along what was proclaimed to be the Portland Road. It wound upwards through obviously mined ground, and she hoped very much that she wasn't trespassing. That could be embarrassing. Unable to see as much as she would have liked while driving along such a tortuous route—only a small crescent of sand lapped by blue sea—she promised herself a further visit as she turned her attention once more to the road.

She eventually came out at the rear of the golf complex and, much to her surprise, saw a very hot and bothered-looking Mark hurrying along the dusty road. Drawing up beside him, she stopped the car and pushed open the passenger door invitingly.

'Want a lift? You certainly look as though you could use one. What have you been doing? Rooting around in the old mine workings?'

'What old mine workings?'

'Back there,' she explained, waving her hand vaguely behind her.

'Oh, no, I didn't know there were any.' And, his mind still clearly on his own problems, his face flushed and sweaty, his dark hair plastered wetly to his forehead, he demanded, 'Are you going near the cliff-top?'

'I can do.'

'Thanks,' he muttered as he climbed in beside her.

'Fed up?' she asked with a compassionate smile as she set the car in motion.

'Yeah. It's that blasted woman!' he burst out crossly.

'Which blasted woman? Clarissa? I thought she was away.'

'Only for a few hours. And do you know what she did?' he demanded. 'She bloody shopped me.'

'Oh, dear. What did she shop you for?'

'Nothing! I wasn't doing *anything*!'

'Ah, the worst kind of shopping there is,' Jenna agreed sagely.

He stared at her, then gave a reluctant grin. 'Well, I wasn't. There was this bird, right? It had been blown against the cliff, and I thought its wing might be broken or something, and all I was doing was leaning over to try and see!'

'And Clarissa saw you?' she guessed. 'And, because you aren't supposed to be scrambling over cliffs with your broken arm, she told your brother?'

'Yeah. And I never tell on *her*!'

'Don't you?' she asked sympathetically. 'And what does *she* do that might need shopping?'

'Lies!' he said forcefully. 'She tells people she's his personal assistant, that he confides in her, that she looks after all his concerns. And she doesn't! She helps with his research—that's all! And Bay would be furious if he knew. But did I tell him? No, I didn't, because when his mind is on his writing, when he's in the middle of a book, I don't disturb him, ever! Because I know it breaks his concentration,' he added virtuously.

'But Clarissa obviously doesn't abide by the same rules. And she told him about you?'

'Yes! And because he wasn't really paying attention, because he didn't want to even *know*, he said I was grounded. It isn't fair!'

'Grounded is being made to stay in?' she queried gently.

'Yes!'

'So what, my friend, are you doing out? Flouting the rules?'

He turned such a woebegone face towards her, gave her such a look of hurt entreaty, that she wanted to hug him. Thirteen was such an awful age. 'Well, I had to, didn't I? The bird might be *dying* for all anybody cares!'

'And is that where you're going now?'

'Yes,' he admitted defiantly.

'Need a hand? A bit of inexpert advice? I could hang on to your ankles or something while you lean over,' she suggested, knowing full well that if she didn't go with him he would go anyway, and she could hardly forbid him, seeing as it was absolutely nothing to do with her, but if she did accompany him, well, at least she could prevent him doing anything too foolhardy.

'Would you? Really?'

'Sure; I don't have any really pressing engagements at the moment.' She wasn't sure he entirely understood her irony, but he gave her a grateful smile.

When they pulled up on the cliff-top, ventured to the edge of the cliff, lay, and leaned perilously over, it was to find that the bird—if, in fact, it was the same bird—far from being in need of rescue, was complacently preening itself. It turned its head when they peered over, blinked one indifferent eye, and took off.

'Well, there's gratitude!' Jenna exclaimed. 'Here we've been tearing about the countryside on a hot afternoon, setting ourselves up for harsh punishment from a wicked elder brother whose rules we've just flouted, and the wretched bird doesn't even have the decency to be injured! Doesn't even bother to say thank you! I really don't know what's happening to younger birds nowadays,' she murmured disgustedly as she scrambled backwards. 'No standards, that's what it is. Haven't been brought up properly if you ask me.'

'A statement which could be equally well applied to a certain young lady who's been aiding and abetting the flouting,' Bay drawled quietly from behind them. He didn't sound entirely amused.

From her prone position, and with a determination that she was *not* going to be affected by him any more, she twisted her head to look up at him, and her silly heart turned over. His dark hair was attractively ruffled by the breeze off the sea, his eyes looked bluer, his face browner. Why, she wondered despairingly, why did he have this effect on her? Especially when she didn't *want* him to!

Quite unaware that her face was smudged with dirt, that her topknot had come rather charmingly unravelled, that she looked very little older than Mark, she sighed. More pretending to do. 'Caught red-handed,' she murmured. 'Now isn't that just my luck? Incarceration? Diet of bread and water?'

'At the very least,' he agreed almost absently as he turned his gaze on his brother. 'I won't ask why you didn't tell me of your need to flout rules laid down for your own protection,' he stated quietly, 'because we are both well aware that I would not have been listening. I will not even give you a scolding for disobeying a ruling that I wasn't even aware I was making. What I will scold you for is worrying Clarissa. I did ask, if you remember, that if you couldn't show her affection, then you could at least try for a little common courtesy.'

'I did show her courtesy! If she said I didn't, then she's lying!' he exclaimed as he scrambled to his feet.

'Is she? You didn't tell her that she was stupid?'

'No!' When his brother merely raised one eyebrow, he flushed darkly, and muttered, 'Well, she wouldn't listen, said I wasn't to go out again. And I *had* to! You surely didn't expect me to leave a dying bird to—die!'

'Does sound unreasonable, doesn't it?'

'Yes!'

'However——'

'I know, I know,' he muttered. 'If I'd stayed away from the cliff in the first place, as I was supposed to, I wouldn't have seen the bird——'

'Correct. Now go on back to the villa and apologise to Clarissa,' he ordered quietly.

'Oh, Bay,' he sighed. 'Do I have to?'

'Yes.'

'But she——' One glance from blue-green eyes was enough to make him break off. His mouth tight, he glared at his brother, then stalked off.

'And as for you,' Bay continued as he held out an absent hand to help her up, 'I would be extraordinarily grateful if you wouldn't encourage him. Clarissa's job is hard enough without you making it ten times worse. Don't you think that as a friend of his you have some sort of responsibility towards him? I know—who better?—how volatile he is, but he likes you, admires you, and urging him to flout rules laid down for his own protection...'

'I did not urge him,' she corrected him, her eyes fixed on his. 'And blaming Clarissa's obviously bad handling of the incident on me is highly unfair.'

'Is it? Yet until he met you there *was* no bad handling, because no rules were flouted.'

'And you really think it's my fault?' Still staring at him, searching his eyes, which remained so steady, she asked, 'How long has Clarissa been with you?'

'A few months.'

'Then you don't think that it might just possibly be a build-up of Clarissa's meddling . . .?'

'No,' he denied unequivocally. 'She doesn't meddle. At my behest, she keeps an eye on him, provides a calming influence. And you, Miss Draycott, can hardly be said to do that. He's a very impressionable young man.'

'Meaning?'

'Meaning Clarissa is—homely. She has none of your advantages. Wealth, upbringing, whatever, and because you are beautiful, can afford to indulge a lifestyle that obviously pleases you, naturally Mark will make comparisons. He isn't yet old enough to judge fairly. You can afford to be nice to him, flatter him— not difficult to understand, then, that he prefers to listen to you rather than Clarissa. You have everything she does not.'

'I see.'

'Good, and I've seen firsthand what wealth can do to a young impressionable mind, and although I do not say that you indulge yourself to excess——'

'Kind of you,' she said acidly.

He inclined his head in acknowledgement. 'I do not want Mark to grow up thinking that money and good looks are the answer to all life's little ills, or that people who don't have them aren't worth bothering with.'

'And you think that those are the standards I'm giving him?'

'Not deliberately, no; I'm just asking you not to take his side against Clarissa, or encourage him to treat her with a contempt she does not deserve.' With another little nod, he turned and walked away.

'Mr Rawson,' she called, and when he stopped and turned she countered quietly, 'The same could be said of you. Wealthy, attractive...'

He gave a cynical smile. 'I work, Miss Draycott.'

So did she. But it was hardly his fault if he didn't know that. And all because she'd been trying to keep him at a distance, pretend she didn't find him attractive, she was now to be blamed for his brother's disobedience? She had deliberately fostered the impression that she was lightweight, originally because of his assumptions, and because she'd thought it might be fun, then because she had begun to like him and hadn't wanted him to know that she did, because of his warnings, because she'd been confused and muddled and vulnerable... And now that she'd succeeded in giving him a totally wrong impression she didn't like that either. Never satisfied, are you, Jenna? she thought wryly.

'Perhaps you should head off to Monte Carlo, or Cannes,' he said softly as she passed him on her way back to her car. 'I'm sure you must have acquaintances there with villas you could—borrow.'

Halting, she stared at him in confusion, then remembered that she'd told him Helen had lent her the villa; not rented—lent. 'No, no,' she replied with a glimmering smile. 'I've already been there this year. Perhaps Martinique.' It was becoming quite horrifying the way these glib explanations just tripped off her tongue.

Climbing into her car, she drove on to her villa.
And now he would think even more badly of her, and
that wasn't fair, because she didn't think badly of him,
despite his rotten assumptions. And what sort of lifestyle did he have, with his firsthand knowledge of
young minds being spoiled by wealth? Obviously one
a great deal different from her own. And he was the
same as all the rest, wasn't he—appearing to be one
thing, then turning out to be something else? Just like
David. And that hurt.

CHAPTER SIX

JENNA didn't feel like going down to the restaurant, talking to people, being cheerful, so she made herself a snack and then lay on the sofa to watch television. Fourteen channels to choose from—that should keep her mind occupied, shouldn't it?

At ten, fed up with herself, fed up with her contradictory behaviour, she switched off the television, then just sat staring at the wall. Ever since the accident she hadn't been like herself at all. It was as though she had gone away and left someone else in her place. Maybe it would be best to go home. Perhaps in familiar surroundings she would revert to being Jenna.

Taking her plate and cup out to the kitchen, she debated going out for a drink. It might help her sleep, might help distract her mind from Bay, from regret and disappointment.

Without giving herself further time to think, she quickly tidied herself, snatched up her car keys and bag, and went out to her car. She'd go down to the Piano Bar, she decided, listen to the American pianist that everyone was talking about.

Small—intimate, she mentally corrected. 'Small' was mundane; 'intimate' conjured up a much more superior image. It was also dark, with awkwardly placed mirrors which she found extraordinarily disconcerting. She kept getting odd glimpses of herself from angles she never normally saw. Embarrassing rather than gratifying. It was also crowded, and she smiled vaguely at people as she made her way to the bar.

Perched on a high stool, she sipped her drink and watched people in the mirror behind the optics, and then stiffened as she saw Bay come in—and knew that telling herself she no longer liked him was a lie. And why? she wondered, almost despairingly. Why this man—this one man above all others? A man who was unobtainable. His dark hair was untidy; he was attractive, certainly, but his face wasn't in any way remarkable. And yet, just by looking at him, you knew he was different; knew he was someone special. When he saw her here, as he no doubt would, would he still think she was chasing him? Even though she'd been here first?

He was obviously well-known—although well-known as a celebrity perhaps, not necessarily as a friend. People smiled at him, nudged each other when he passed by, and either he was totally oblivious to their whispering or preferred to ignore it. He returned people's smiles and nods, but not in a way that would invite conversation. Not warmly, as he had once smiled at her. But not any more. He caught sight of her as he made his way to the bar and, because fate was probably playing games, the only gap where he could stand to order a drink was beside her. He didn't even hesitate, which could only mean that her presence didn't bother him in the slightest.

'Hello, Jenna,' he greeted her casually, and then turned to smile at the barman as he hurried up.

'Scotch?'

'Please,' Bay agreed as he idly scanned the people around him. Then, presumably spotting the person he'd been looking for, he picked up his drink and his change and began to move away. 'Excuse me; someone I have to see.'

'Yes, of course,' Jenna said quietly.

A very attractive woman barred his way with the obvious intention of flirting, but he just gave his economical smile and moved round her, only to halt when the barman attracted his attention. 'Clarissa's just come in,' he said quietly. 'I think she's looking for you.'

Jenna also turned to watch as the other girl began threading her way towards them, curious to see how she behaved with Bay, and was disappointed to find that she seemed to behave no differently than she had with herself.

'Clarissa?' he greeted her with some surprise. 'Is something wrong?'

'It's Mark,' she whispered. 'I can't find him.' Chewing worriedly on her bottom lip, her eyes fixed on Bay, she exclaimed distractedly, 'I don't know where else to look!'

'How long has he been gone?'

'Hours! I've driven round the complex, rung all the people I thought might have seen him, but he just didn't come back!'

'Back from where?' he asked with a frown. 'I thought he was staying in.'

'So did I! And I don't know back from where, I just meant . . . wherever he'd gone. I blame myself utterly!' she exclaimed as she began to wind one long piece of hair agitatedly round and round her finger. 'How could I not know he wasn't in his room? How could I not have checked? How——'

'Clarissa,' he interrupted. 'Don't.'

'Yes. But——'

Holding up his hand to halt the flow, he put his glass on a convenient table and threaded his way towards the piano, Clarissa hovering worriedly behind him. He had a quiet word with the pianist, who promptly broke off what he was playing and asked over the microphone if anyone had seen Mark Rawson. There was a chorus of noes, and then several offers to help look for him.

Within minutes, a search party had been assembled, and Jenna quietly joined their number.

'You're intending to help look?' Bay asked in obvious amazement.

'Yes, of course. Why on earth wouldn't I?' she demanded.

'No reason, I suppose,' he conceded. 'I was just surprised, that's all.' Turning away from her, he began to organise the others.

Glancing at Clarissa, who was standing beside her, and watching her with a rather dubious air, Jenna raised her eyebrows in query.

'Oh, sorry,' she apologised, sounding flustered, 'I didn't mean to stare; it's just that you're so pretty.'

A bit nonplussed, Jenna murmured faintly, 'Oh, thank you.'

'And I'm sure Bay didn't mean to—well... you know... Oh, I think we're off.'

No, I don't know! Jenna wanted to exclaim, but Clarissa was already moving away. Frustrated, and wishing the wretched girl would finish one sentence before beginning on another, she followed everyone else outside.

'Jenna,' Bay called as she walked towards her car, 'I'll meet you up on the top road. You'd better change

first,' he added as he took in the soft flowery skirt
she was wearing.

'Right.' Obviously the reprimand of earlier was to
be forgotten. Climbing into her car, she drove back
to the villa, quickly changed into cotton trousers and
a T-shirt, then drove up to the top road. Bay was
already there with several other men and she parked
and went to join them.

'Got a torch?' he demanded.

'Oh, no. Sorry, I didn't think——'

'Never mind,' he cut in impatiently, 'use mine.'
Thrusting it into her hand, he continued briskly,
waving one hand towards the cliff on their left. 'Right,
this is your area of search. George and——'

'Couldn't I do the road?' she asked worriedly, 'I'm
not sure I could clamber over the cliff-top...'

He looked astonished, as well he might, she
thought, but no way could she go clambering over the
cliff-top with her bad leg, no matter how much she
might want to.

'Your knee's all right now, isn't it?'

'Well, yes...'

'Then I can't see what the problem is. Anyway,
other people are doing the roads, and if he falls over
the damned cliff because we were here arguing the
finer points of search... You'll have George to your
left and Alberto to the right. If you see anything, just
shout.'

'Yes, but I really don't think I can do the cliffs!'
she exclaimed urgently as he began to walk away.

Swinging back to face her, he stared at her in disbelief. 'Can't?'

'No. There's all those bushes and rocks, and I...'

Before she could finish, explain why she couldn't
do it, he strode back and stared at her with an expression she had not seen on his face before. Granite
would have looked warmer. 'My young brother is
missing, possibly injured,' he said in the same tone
of disbelief. 'You offered, which I have to confess
surprised me, but having offered, and been desig-
nated a search area, it's now too late to recall someone
else to take your place! I don't ask much of people,
but I am asking this, and I thought, obviously stupidly, that your offer was genuinely meant!'

With an exasperated sigh, and hardly comforted by
knowing all this misunderstanding was her own fault,
she supposed she could *try*. She didn't think she would
be much use, but if something awful happened to
Mark because of her inability to clamber over rocks
she'd never forgive herself... And why didn't he ask
much of people? Because of pride? Or because in the
past people had fallen sadly short of his expectations—as she had done? Because he thought she
swanned off to other people's villas in exotic places,
and because she was a bad influence on his brother.
Or was it because she was like Maureen, who was
clever? Whoever Maureen was. And none of which
was important at the moment.

The torch-beam swinging wildly, she limped across
the road and scrambled awkwardly through the bushes
that led to the cliff-top, then hauled herself up the
gradient. She could see other lights in the distance,
hear shouts, but none near enough to identify. Eyeing
the bumpy and rocky headland with despair, and
praying that Mark was nowhere near here, for his own
sake, she used a spiky bush to pull herself up the

slippery scree. She called tentatively, shone her torch around, and slowly made her way towards the cliff.

If she just managed to search the edge, make sure he hadn't fallen over, that would be best, wouldn't it. She'd never get up and down all the gullies, round every bush and shrub. Feeling utterly useless, and full of misgivings, praying she wouldn't turn her good ankle, she peered into the gully before her, shone her torch into the depths.

'God Almighty!' Bayne exploded from behind her, nearly making her fall over in fright. 'We're looking for a boy, not a bloody cat! It's no good hovering on the edge; get down and search the damned thing properly.'

'I can't...'

'Why not?' he demanded scathingly. 'Afraid of chipping your bloody nail-varnish?'

'No, I'm not and stop making so many damned assumptions! I told you I wouldn't be very good at clambering round rocks and shrubs in the dark. I did offer to drive round the roads...'

'I don't need you to drive round the roads,' he in- sisted savagely. 'The older people are doing that, those genuinely incapable of clambering over cliff-tops!'

'But I am genuinely incapable of——'

'Compassion! Yes, so I already discovered!' he broke in disgustedly. 'Oh, go back to your villa; we'll no doubt manage perfectly well without you!' Wrenching the torch off her, he added cuttingly, 'Sy- barites can sometimes be amusing companions, es- pecially when they're pretty! Tonight, sybarites are no damned use whatsoever!' Making sure he had his balance, he began to slide into the gully.

Sybarite? Yes, because she had not corrected his impressions. But what she had not given him was the impression that she was totally selfish! Even allowing for his worry over Mark, it was still a damnable thing to say.

Hurt, and, yes, angry, because she had never given him reason to believe that she wished his brother anything but good, she turned away. With no torch to light her way back, and afraid of falling, she made her way gingerly down towards the road. He'd given her absolutely no chance to explain... Well, to hell with it. You could be so *wrong* about people! So why continue to imbue people with qualities they clearly don't have? she asked herself scathingly. Sybarite! Perhaps that was what the unknown Maureen was! Perhaps they wore the same colour nail-varnish!

If you'd told him about your leg before, the misunderstanding would never have arisen, a little inner voice whispered. But she hadn't wanted to tell him. Hadn't wanted to tell anyone, because if you explained one thing you had to explain others, because people were never satisfied with simple explanations, and to have explained fully—well, it would have been embarrassing. But she could have told him, couldn't she, that she had a weak leg? That would have had no need of explanation. So why hadn't she? Because she *had* wanted to help. Had wanted to shine in his eyes? Perhaps. And that had to be the most idiotic reasoning of all time, because she'd really shone now, hadn't she? Always willing to give the benefit of the doubt to others, she stupidly expected the compliment to be returned. And that made her the fool, as she was often being a fool. Own fault, Jenna, yes, but she hadn't wanted him to *dislike* her, only wanted

him to think that she was bent on a light flirtation . . .
Hadn't wanted him to know how he could make her
feel.

Using the bushes for support, she eventually
managed to get back to the road. A car was just
cruising past, and the man driving stopped beside her.
'Any luck?'

'No, afraid not. Bayne's taken over my area of
search,' she explained defensively, and then wished
she hadn't bothered. It was nothing to do with anyone
else after all.

'You want a lift back anywhere?' he asked kindly.
'You look as though you've hurt yourself. Rick your
ankle, did you? That's the trouble,' he continued.
'Even with a torch, you can't see all the damned rocks
and holes. Come on, hop in.'

Before she could explain that she had her own car,
a low shout went up from their right and they both
turned to look in that direction. 'Sounds like they
might have found him!' he exclaimed in relief.

'Yes,' Jenna agreed, her eyes narrowing on several
bobbing flashlights as at least two people hurried towards where the shout had come from. Uncons-
ciously crossing her fingers, she strained both ears and
eyes until she made out the small, trudging figure of
Mark. With a little exclamation, she began limping
towards him. Ignoring the questions being hurled at
him that he was quite clearly incapable of answering,
she put a comforting arm round his shoulder. In the
torchlight being shone in his face, she saw the grubby
traces of tears.

'Are you all right?' she asked gently.

'Yeah, I——'

'Hurt anywhere?' one of the other men interrupted.

'No—I fell down a hole,' he blurted, 'and I couldn't get out, and I thought...' Swallowing hard, he gave a little shudder.

'Shh, shh,' Jenna soothed. 'You're safe now.' Glancing at her companions, she said quietly, 'Someone had better let Bay know.'

'Yes, I wi—— Oh, hell!' one of them suddenly exclaimed comically, under his breath. 'I definitely will, before the dreaded Clarissa gets here!'

Turning her head, Jenna watched the other girl hurry towards them. 'Don't you like her?' she asked quietly.

'No.' George grinned. 'Isn't it dreadful? She's probably extremely nice; she *means* well!' he explained comically. 'And I know exactly what will happen. She'll blame herself—she always does, whether it be for the weather or a multiple pile-up on the motorway that she was nowhere near.' With a little pat on her arm, he hurried away, and with a great deal more haste than tact was followed by the two other people who'd been with them. Which meant what? That Bay was the only one who didn't see Clarissa as she really was?

'Was that George?' Clarissa queried, peering rather myopically after one of the men.

'I've no idea,' Jenna said lamely. 'I——'

'Oh, Mark,' Clarissa reproached as she turned her attention away from Jenna. 'Where on earth have you been?' And without waiting for an answer she ploughed on. 'Just look at the state of you! Whatever will your brother say? So thoughtless, all the trouble you've caused——'

'I didn't——' Mark began, only to be interrupted.

'If only you would *think*! Well, I blame myself! If only I had kept a closer eye on you, none of this would have happened.'

'It's not your——' Mark began indignantly.

'Somewhat impossible, I should have thought, with a boy as lively and adventurous as Mark,' Jenna interrupted quietly and with a warning squeeze of Mark's shoulder. 'And so long as he's safe, no one will mind having turned out.'

'That's not the point,' she reproved gently. 'If he would only learn to think before he acts——'

'I did think!' Mark said savagely. 'And it's nothing to do with you!' Wrenching himself free of Jenna's hold, and trying to disguise his little sob, he began to hurry along the road.

'Oh, dear,' she mourned. 'He's so headstrong. Such a worry for Bay, as he won't tell him off, you know...' Shaking her head, as though the ways of the world were quite incomprehensible to her, she began to follow him and Jenna could hear her voice monotonously bemoaning his selfishness. She saw Bay's tall figure run down the bank to intercept him, saw the hug he briefly gave him, and turned away. With a tired sigh, she began to limp down to where her car was parked. Did Bay really think that Clarissa was a calming influence on his brother? Was he really that blind? Apparently he was. Homely; and filled with good intentions. A sure recipe for disaster where someone like Mark was concerned—and absolutely no business of Jenna's. The way she was feeling about Bay at the moment, he was welcome to her. She might blame herself for the world's ills, but she presumably wasn't a sybarite.

It seemed an awful effort to get ready for bed and, when she had settled herself, Jenna found she couldn't sleep. Her mind, working independently of her tired body, continued to brood about what Bay had said. Sybarite. Not an on-the-spot judgement, but what he had obviously thought from the moment he'd met her. Or only since they'd come back from Albacete? Not that it mattered when he'd thought it. Or did sensualist *mean* sybarite? She'd have to look it up.

'Sybarites can sometimes be amusing companions,' that was what he'd said. Not someone he'd met and liked, but someone he viewed with amused derision, or even contempt. Not very nice. Not entirely his fault, she supposed drearily, because she had deliberately tried to give him the impression of someone only wanting to top up her tan. But sybarite? No.

Lying on top of the covers, tossing and turning, not only because her mind was active, but because of the heat and the humidity that had been building up all evening, she eventually stripped off her damp nightie, and when that didn't work, when she still felt no cooler, she got up to get herself a cold drink. Her leg ached, a dull pain in her calf, nagging, and she just wanted to sleep, forget it all. Grabbing a bottle of pain-killers, she defiantly took two—which was why, when she did get back to bed, she slept right through the violent storm that raged for at least four hours.

'Jenna!'

When the shout was repeated, accompanied by a violent shake of her shoulder, she reluctantly opened her eyes and stared with dulled senses at Bay. Bay? Blinking the sleep from her eyes, she stared up at him in astonishment. 'What are you doing in my bedroom?' she demanded stupidly.

'What the hell do you think?' he bit out tersely. 'And why in God's name didn't you put the shutters down?'

'Shutters?'

'Yes! Shutters! Didn't you hear the damned storm?'

'Storm?'

'For Pete's sake! Will you stop repeating everything I say and get up!'

She started to sit up, remembered she was naked, and hastily clutched the covers to her. And why on earth did he sound so savage? Hastily averting her eyes from a face filled with such incomprehensible anger, she noticed the yukka plant. The yukka plant that was floating jauntily no more than a foot from her bed. Floating?

Jerking upright, she stared in disbelief at the foliage that yesterday had been standing artistically beside the bookshelf in the lounge. This morning it was floating in the sea of muddy water that surrounded her.

CHAPTER SEVEN

JENNA closed her eyes, then opened them again. Still there. Oh, good grief. And although it was a shock it was somehow a forced consciousness, an almost desperate attempt to ignore Bay's very disturbing presence in her bedroom; to ignore the moody look on his face, the tension that had firmed his muscles; to forget the fact that she was naked beneath the light cover, which made her feel extraordinarily vulnerable, and tense.

'Did a pipe burst?' she asked stupidly, still frowning down at the water.

'No, a pipe did not burst! Now will you please get up and let's get the hell out of here?'

Switching her gaze to him, then hastily away, she repeated, 'Out of here?'

'Yes, Jenna,' he said with heavy patience, 'out of here. And how the hell you managed to sleep through a storm that had to be the most violent on record defies comprehension!'

Barely listening, still a bit muzzy headed from the pain-killers, she watched him wade round to the window and drag back the curtains. Stared at his naked back—and fervently prayed he would go away. Wished she weren't so conscious of long brown legs exposed by his cut-off jeans, of a smooth brown chest... Wrenching her eyes away as he turned to look at her, she pretended a fascinated interest in the progress of the yukka plant. Still frowning down at it, she absently pushed her long hair off her face, then saw that her robe had slipped over the side of the bed and was trailing in the water. Rolling over, she gingerly picked it up between finger and thumb. She heard Bay give an exclamation, and turned her head to find him staring down at the long, jagged scar on her foot. Hastily withdrawing it, she glared at him.

'What happened to it?' he asked almost accusingly.

'I cut it.'

'How?'

'Does it matter?' she asked stiffly.

'No,' he denied quietly. 'But you don't get a cut like that by just treading on something. When did you do it?'

'A few months ago.'

'And is that why you were unable to clamber about on cliff-tops?'

'Yes.'

'Then why the hell didn't you say so?' he demanded angrily. 'And will you please get up?'

Her mouth tight, she ostentatiously pulled the cover more securely around her. 'I'll get up when you've gone. And you hardly gave me a chance to tell you anything!'

'No,' he agreed moodily, 'I didn't, did I? Is that what this is all about? You think I owe you an apology? All right,' he agreed. 'I was probably out of order.'

'You were definitely out of order!'

'I was worried about Mark.'

'That doesn't give you the right to call me names.'

'No, it doesn't. I'm sorry.'

'Apology accepted,' she said in the same distant tone he was using. But it wasn't accepted, and it couldn't be forgotten, because his apology had hardly been unqualified. And will you please go away? she silently begged him. 'How is Mark?'

'Fine. A few cuts and bruises,' he explained impatiently. 'They've kept him in the hospital overnight just to be sure there's no concussion.'

'What happened to him?'

His face clearly mirroring his exasperation, he said flatly, 'He apparently fell down one of the old mine workings along the Portland Road. It took him several hours to get himself out again. All right? Can we go now?'

'Mine workings?' Dear God, had he investigated them because she'd told him about them? 'I think——' she began guiltily, only to be interrupted.

'Jenna!' he warned savagely. 'Will you get the hell out of this bed before I tip you out?'

'No! and will you stop ordering me about? Go where?' she demanded as she remembered what he'd said.

'To my villa, of course. You can't stay here!'

'Don't be ridiculous; I'm not a child; of course I can stay here. Anyway, I can't leave the place like this!'

'The maintenance people will see to it . . .'

'I imagine they have quite enough to do if everyone else is in the same boat . . .' Realising what she had said, the unintentional pun, she looked away. She didn't find it even remotely funny.

'Oh, no,' he denied with a brief unamused laugh, 'only you. You were apparently the only idiot who didn't hear the storm, the only idiot who didn't put the shutters across the door-sills to keep the water out!'

'Then I'm sure *you* have other important things to do!' she said desperately.

'I do, and stop being so damned pompous.'

'Sybarites are always pompous,' she retorted, feeling goaded.

'Oh, shut up. Just get up and collect your things together.'

'No. I'll get up when you've gone.'

He sighed, gave an exasperated oath, and grabbed the corner of the duvet and tried to yank it off. Jenna held grimly on to her end. 'Don't do that!'

'Stop playing games! I've had no sleep! I'm extraordinarily irritated, which——'

'Why haven't you had any sleep?'

'Because I spent half the night at the hospital,' he gritted, 'and then, when I heard the storm warning, I drove back here to put up the shutters! After that it hardly seemed worth going to bed! Consequently, I'm not in the best of tempers, and I am not about to play silly games with you! Now let go! Modesty hardly becomes you at this late stage!' He gave another tug, and Jenna tugged back, obviously harder than expected, and because he was wedged between the window and the bed, because there was no room for him to manoeuvre, he overbalanced and sat heavily on the mattress, narrowly missing her bad leg.

'Watch what you're doing, you fool!' she exclaimed, almost able to *feel* the pain that would have ensued if he'd landed on her.

His face grim, his jaw gritted, because he did not know what he might have done, he got a firmer grip on the cover and, in temper, wrenched it out of her hold. Then he froze, and quickly tossed it back. 'Why in God's name didn't you say you didn't have anything on?'

'Why the hell should I?' Mortified, she tucked it securely across her breasts. 'Now go away.' Unbearably conscious of him sitting there, half off, half on the bed, aware of his continued stillness, she refused to look at him, and could only imagine the expression he had on his face. The sort of look a man gave a sybarite? One brown hand still lay near her, long-fingered, strong-looking, and when it slowly moved she said thickly, 'Don't.'

'Don't what?' he asked, his own voice deep and husky. 'And don't try to pretend it isn't what you want, any more than I intend to——'

'It isn't,' she managed, and wished she didn't sound so strangled, wished she could think of something to say. 'What do you mean, you don't intend to?' she demanded in shock.

'Don't play the fool!' he castigated angrily. 'You know perfectly well how you make me feel!'

'I do not! You never said——'

'Of course I didn't. You think I wanted to give you more ammunition?'

'Ammunition?'

'Yes! Why else would I be forever in your garden? To pass the time of *day*?'

Staring at him as though mesmerised, unbelievably shocked, she weakly shook her head.

'First you seem to be one thing,' he muttered, 'then another. Blow hot, then cold...'

'No!'

'Yes. You're just like Maureen, aren't you?' he asked. He sounded bitterly disgusted.

'I don't *know*, do I?' she raged desperately. 'I don't know who Maureen *is*!'

'Someone like you,' he said flatly, distantly, almost absently as he curled his fingers over the edge of the cover, tried to ease it aside. When she refused to release it, his hand moved up towards her chin. With his thumb, he forced her to look at him. 'Just who the hell are you, Jenna?'

'No one. Please go away,' she begged agitatedly.

'Yes, it's what I should do, isn't it?' he asked slowly. 'Because getting embroiled with someone like you will only complicate an already complicated life. Only you aren't an easy lady to put aside——'

'I'm not a book!'

'No, but you are extraordinarily lovely, to look at anyway, and ever since I first saw you in that black swimsuit... Hormones are damnable things, aren't they?'

'How would I know?' she demanded furiously. 'You've just finished intimating that I don't have any!'

'Have I? Even if I misjudged you in Albacete, I still can't get out of my mind the way you made me feel.' His eyes on hers, a rather bleak expression in their depths, he slid his hand round to her nape and pulled her towards him. To her shame, she made only a token resistence as he touched his mouth to hers. It was like being burned. Softly at first, almost tentatively, and then with urgency, as though everything was just too damned much all of a sudden. Then, somehow, he was beside her, and the duvet wasn't tangled about her any more; his warm brown leg had replaced it, and his ragged shorts were no barrier at all.

He covered her fully, fit his strong frame to hers. There weren't any words—there was no time for any—no thought given to their utterance, just a sensual exchange, touch and retreat, move; no time even to de-

light in warm, soft, heated skin as his mouth took
hers in urgent assurance, exquisite skill.

His thumbs probed the hollow beneath her jaw, unbelievably arousing, and she felt a flood of warmth
inside. It was almost dream-like, pre-ordained, and
he was so unbelievably gentle despite the urgency, the
hunger—unbelievably practised, she supposed in the
dim recesses of her consciousness as he touched his
hands to her exquisite shape. Soothed, warmed, excited; she wasn't totally inexperienced, but no man
had ever made her feel like this. Not wanting it to
ever end. Wanting to excite him as he excited her with
no thoughts of tomorrow, no thought for anything
but pleasing him, being pleased. They moved about
the bed like some strange ballet as they urgently
touched one another. And then they heard her call.

'Bay?'

'Oh, my God,' he groaned. 'Clarissa. What the hell
is she doing back?'

'Back?' Jenna asked blankly.

'Yes. I left her at the hospital.' Galvanised into
action, he got up, dragged on his shorts, then just
stared at her. 'It will be best if she doesn't find me
here.'

'Will it? Why? Because Clarissa is more to you than
you said?'

'No!'

Hurt, not really knowing what she was saying, only
needing to say something, now that emotion was
spent, feeling empty, she stared up at him. He
looked—guilty, as though afraid of being caught in
a compromising situation, and the abrupt change from
ardent lover was shattering, mortifying. It had not
seemed wrong, only beautiful; now it seemed—sordid.

She heard Clarissa call again, closer, and the full realisation of what she had done, what she had allowed him to do, washed over her. 'Go away!'

'I can't leave you like this!'

'Of course you can leave me like this! It's what you intended, isn't it?'

'I didn't intend anything at all,' he denied grimly.

'Didn't you? Why? Because I'm a sybarite? Or because of Maureen?'

'Mareen?' he echoed.

'Yes,' she hissed. 'The Maureen *I* mustn't mention but everyone else can!'

His face changed, became bleak, confirmation, had she needed it, that Maureen was something other than a past mistress.

'Oh, go away, get out of here! We don't want to put Clarissa's nose out of joint, do we?' she taunted bitterly. Unable to look at him any more, she rolled away, dragged the duvet across her and put one arm over her eyes. 'Just go,' she said thickly. 'If you think anything of me at all,' she added fiercely, 'just go.' Go, she silently urged him. Please, please, just go.

She could feel him watching her, still and silent, thinking—what? Then Clarissa called again from somewhere out front, and he quietly left. Out through the lounge and into the back garden. Would he walk round the front? Evince surprise at seeing Clarissa? Tightening the arm across her face, she shut her eyes and ears tight.

When she'd gained some semblance of control, she uncovered her eyes and stared up at the ceiling through a blur of tears. Oh, Jenna, you fool. You stupid little fool, she thought. Now she must leave. And if he *was* involved with Clarissa? Then she would not be able to face her, either.

Only the gods hadn't finished with her; they wanted to twist the knife. She'd just rolled into a sitting position, the quilt huddled round her, when she heard the swish of footsteps through the lounge. Clarissa. Still calling. Closing her eyes in defeat, Jenna waited. Perhaps if no one answered... A wasted thought because two minutes later Clarissa waded in.

'Oh!' she exclaimed inadequately. 'Sorry. I was looking for Bay. I thought he said he was coming down to see if you were all right. Are you?' she asked somewhat dubiously.

'Yes,' Jenna managed, keeping her eyes down.

'Has he been here?'

'No.' Feeling at a distinct disadvantage, she wriggled to the edge of the bed and put her feet over the side—straight into the cold, muddy water.

'You should have put your shutters across the doors,' she stated unnecessarily.

'Yes.'

'It's an awful mess...' Her gaze sharpening, Clarissa stared down into the water, then bent and picked something up. 'This is Bay's little recorder,' she exclaimed with a frown. 'He always takes it with him for notes and things.' Staring back at Jenna, she accused, 'You said he hadn't been here.'

'Yes,' Jenna admitted helplessly.

She stared at Jenna, and then slowly round the room.

'He's not here now,' Jenna told her listlessly, and quite unnecessarily.

'No.' Awkwardly holding the recorder out, Clarissa muttered, 'Perhaps you'd like to give it back to him.

I mean, if I do, he'll know that I... And it really...
I don't know what to say.'

'No,' Jenna agreed gently as she took the recorder
and put it beside her on the bed. 'Neither do I.'

'I'd better go. I'm really sorry if I... that I——'

'It doesn't matter,' Jenna interrupted. 'Really.'

Obviously relieved at not having to discuss it,
Clarissa added in a bright tone that deceived nobody,
'Although I am glad that I've seen you on your own,
because I think I may owe you an apology.'

'Do you? Why? Look, do you mind if I get
dressed?' Jenna asked desperately.

'Oh, no, please go ahead.' Virtuously averting her
gaze as Jenna dragged herself, quilt and all, over to
the small dressing-table and took out trousers, a pair
of shorts and a T-shirt and quickly tugged them on,
she continued, 'I think I said something I shouldn't,
and so I'm really glad to be able to explain.'

Oh, dear heaven. Clarissa, Clarissa, if the gods ever
ask you what you want, beg for some intuition. 'Explain what?' Jenna asked tiredly.

Clarissa stared at her, now decently clad, her eyes
wide behind the horn-rimmed glasses, and Jenna
thought that she really might have been quite pretty
if she had had her hair done differently, worn dif-
ferent-shaped glasses... 'About last night.'

'Yes? What about last night?'

'On the cliff-top. I just said.'

'No, you didn't,' Jenna denied with as much dignity
and patience as she could muster. 'You said you had
to... But you didn't.'

'Oh, well, it was Mrs Braden. You know Mrs
Braden?'

'No.'

'Well, she's a resident here, and she heard Bay shouting at you on the cliff-top, when Mark was missing, and she went on and on about this being a community and everyone helping and everything, and that they didn't want people here who didn't fit in. I said, at least I think I said, that I was sure that Bay hadn't meant what he'd said, because he'd been worried and everything, and that I was sure that you were very nice. Not everyone wants to go tramping round the countryside, do they? I mean *I* didn't.'

'No—but you did,' Jenna pointed out.

'Yes, but that was because it was probably my fault. I was responsible for him, a sort of mothering influence.' She smiled. 'Or that's what Bay says. I should have been keeping a better eye on him, and I just wanted to warn you that some people might be a bit distant with you because they might think you didn't want to help look for Mark. And Bay is very popular here, you know. Well, I expect he's popular everywhere: quite famous and, of course, wealthy, and people do tend to—well, make up to him. I did try to explain that no one would make judgements without knowing the full facts... I mean, being a writer's assistant, that's the first thing you learn: check your facts!'

'Yes,' Jenna agreed inadequately, beginning to feel ever so slightly punch-drunk.

'So I'm glad I've had the chance to explain.'

'Yes. And did you?'

'Did I what?' she asked with some confusion.

'Check your facts?'

'Oh, no—well, I couldn't, could I? But you mustn't be thinking that you were the only one who wouldn't help, because you weren't. But people don't *expect* those people to help because they *know* them! It's because people liked you and they now might think they were misled, if you understand me...'

'Yes,' Jenna agreed lamely. 'Misled. Thank you for explaining.' And now please, please go away.

'You're very welcome,' she said seriously, 'and I did tell Mrs Braden... I do babble on, don't I?'

'Yes.'

'Oh.' Looking confused for a moment, as though she hadn't expected agreement, Clarissa comforted, 'Anyway, I'm sure it isn't *true*!'

'No,' Jenna agreed helplessly.

'No, of course it isn't,' she soothed, as though she were placating a child, 'and now I'd better go. Oh, Bay said you were to come up to the villa—er...that's why he came in the first place. So shall I help you pack?'

Shaking her head, Jenna said quietly, 'No, thank you anyway.'

'All right. And I'll leave you to give Bay his recorder back, shall I?'

'Yes.'

'Right. I'll be off, then. And I'm sorry—well, you know.'

'Yes.'

When she'd gone, Jenna slumped tiredly down on the side of the bed. Go up to his villa? she thought with a hollow laugh. Oh, yes, that was really likely, wasn't it? And if she was going to be ostracised as well, as Clarissa seemed to fear...

With a long shudder, she put her face in her hands. Oh, Jenna, what a fool you are! she moaned silently. And if he was involved with another girl, or this unknown Maureen, then she hated him for cheating. Hatred was just as legitimate an emotion as love. Better to tell herself she hated him. Well, disliked anyway. Because she hadn't been entirely innocent, had she? But she hadn't known he was attracted to her. Really she hadn't. Not like that. Not ...

With another shudder, she got up wearily, dragged her case off the top of the wardrobe and slung it on the bed. Opening the doors, she began transferring her clothes, and when she'd done that she bent to retrieve her shoes, which were floating upside-down in the muddy water. How much more was she supposed to put up with? And it wasn't even ten o'clock yet, she saw. Taking out her sodden shoes, she wrapped them in a plastic bag and shoved them into her case. Taking the rest of the stuff out of the dressing-table, she pushed that in too.

Snapping down the locks, she left her case on the bed and waded along to the bathroom. Not knowing if she should use the water, electricity, or anything else for that matter, she collected up her toiletries and went to clean her teeth with some bottled water from the kitchen.

She made do with a biscuit and a glass of orange juice for breakfast, then swished through to the lounge to see what other damage had been done. The water wasn't very deep, just above her ankles, in fact, but it was cold and there were some rather nasty, unidentifiable bits floating about in it. She stood staring in despair at the altered décor, her mind violently wrenched from her own problems. Wading gingerly across the room, careful not to tread on anything that

would injure her bad foot, she stared out at the garden
that had now become a lake.

Making her way to the front door, she opened it,
and as the water swirled turgidly round her ankles she
stared out over the complex. Water, water, everywhere, and not a drop to drink.

The section of one of the golf-courses that she could
see was now also a lake—and it all looked so absurd
with the sky a bright, cloudless blue. She could see
people at work, beginning to clear the debris, sweep
water from their gardens and walkways, and gave a
sad little sigh.

She stood watching the activity for a moment, then
went to get her case, put it in the car. No use wishing
for things to be different. About to go and get the
rest of her belongings, she was thankful to see the
little maid making her way towards the villa. She
would, no doubt, think it a bit odd that Jenna wished
to rush off the moment the roads were clear, but she
found she no longer cared what people thought.

An hour later, most of the water outside had soaked
away and they were able to sweep the villa's floors
free of the mud and debris. Assured that the maintenance crew would do the rest, she wrapped up Bay's
recorder and gave it to the maid with instructions for
it to be delivered to Mr Rawson. Pressing some pesetas
into the girl's hand, thanking her for all she had done,
Jenna then left, a rather bleak light in her lovely eyes.
She would ring Helen from the first phone she came
to, she decided, then her mother, telling her that she
had decided to see more of Spain; that she would ring
her from wherever she happened to be; ask her to
explain to Uncle John that she felt well enough to

cope with the rigours of driving herself back; promise
to be careful; promise not to overdo things. Because
she had done quite enough already. Not that she would
tell her mother that, of course.

Because Jenna was still upset, unable to get it out
of her mind, and because when she was upset she
didn't feel like doing *anything*, including driving
through strange towns to look at architecture, points
of interest, she took the main highway towards
Barcelona, and then went on into France. When she
reached Cahors, when tiredness was too great to
ignore, she found a little hotel for the night. She then
spent the next morning limping round the old quarter,
and viewed an ancient house where Henry somebody
or other had stayed, one of the English kings certainly, but which one she was unable to discover because the plaque that proudly proclaimed its history
was half obscured by dirt. Apart from that there were
some nice shops, a river, and an old bridge.

Feeling mean, because she hadn't done the town
justice, because she hadn't been in the mood for
sightseeing, and because she just wanted to get home,
she finally headed for the Channel ports and managed
to get herself booked on to the Poole ferry. There were
no cabins available and she dozed on and off all that
long night in one of the chairs.

She arrived in Shepton Mallet just after lunch, tired,
aching, and longing for a long soak in the bath and
a cup of tea. As she pushed through the door of the
little shop that was run by her mother, which sold the
furniture she helped her father restore, she stopped.
Bay was lounging in an exquisite Queen Anne chair,
and he was smiling at something her mother was

saying. That faint, elusive smile, part mocking, part
bland, which depending on her mood, either aggra-
vated or beguiled her. It certainly seemed to be be-
guiling her mother.

CHAPTER EIGHT

JENNA had driven over half of Europe with it going round and round in her head, and she was sick of the confusion, the hurt, the embarrassment. She was sick of the pain in her leg, of not being able to do anything, she was sick of the irrational guilt, and to see Bay lounging there was the last straw. 'What are you doing here?' she demanded wearily.

He gave her an odd look, rose lazily to his feet, and ordered softly, 'Guess.'

'I don't want to guess,' she said mutinously.

'Then don't be a fool.'

A fool? Well, she was undoubtedly that, and it *still* took an extraordinary amount of effort to block out the memories of her behaviour, of her—uninhibited behaviour, and she began to feel hot again, distressed. It was so hard to look at him, be attracted to him, want to touch and be touched—and then remember what had happened. Remember that he had maybe cheated.

Deliberately turning her head away, she stared at her mother. She was leaning rather too nonchalantly against a delicate and extremely valuable side-table that was definitely not made to bear someone's weight, arms folded, a little smile in her eyes. She looked very like her daughter; the fair hair might be greying, the blue eyes perhaps not so bright, but no one could ever take them for other than mother and daughter.

'He came,' she observed with a slightly wicked grin, 'I saw, he conquered.' Moving upright, she held out her arms. 'Welcome home, sweetheart.'

With a slightly twisted smile of her own, Jenna moved towards her, pressed a kiss to her cheek, and returned the hug.

'Tired, darling?'

'Shattered.'

'Case in the car?'

'Mmm.'

'Bay will get it, won't you?' she asked over her daughter's shoulder.

He gave a wry smile and went to do so.

'I like him,' her mother continued as she moved her daughter back so that she could see her face. 'Wickedly attractive—and the devil to know, I imagine.'

'Yes.'

Her mother chuckled. 'How very non-committal. I shall say no more.'

'Yeah?' Jenna queried, knowing how unlikely that was.

'Well . . .'

They smiled at each other, Mrs Draycott with warmth, Jenna with desperation.

'He has spoken to Helen,' she observed portentiously.

'Has he?' Jenna asked with pretended indifference.

'Yes. Been making wretched work of it, darling?'

'So it would seem. Does my face look spited?'

'Very, and it certainly looks as though you've been trying to cut off your nose. Poor old thing,' she commiserated. 'Bay told me what happened.'

'How kind of him. Did he also tell you that he called me a sybarite?' she asked tartly.

'No,' she grinned. 'Did he? How precious. I quite yearn to know him better. Shall I shut up shop? Play chaperon?'

'No,' Jenna refused bluntly, 'you can tell him to go away. I'm going to have a bath.'

'That bad, huh?' she asked with a gentle smile.

'Yes.'

'All right, my darling, but first I shall drape myself elegantly on the *chaise-longue* and hope he calls me one. If he doesn't I shall immediately tell your father.'

Her words might have been light, amusing, but there was concern in her blue eyes as she stared at her daughter, and Jenna was comforted to know that she would never probe. If Jenna wanted a confidante, then that was different. If she didn't her mother would not demand explanations. By the same token, if she told her mother how she had been hurt, there would be war. And she was much too tired for one.

With a grateful smile, she asked, 'Where *is* father?'

'Gone home. He was tired, he said, of the smell of varnish. A lie, of course, because he's gone to wage further war on the family of rabbits who are using his vegetable plot as their own personal larder. I don't know who enjoys the encounters more—him or the rabbits. I'll ring him, let him know you're back safe. Go on, go and have your bath; we can talk later.'

With a tired nod, Jenna pushed open the door at the side of the shop and awkwardly began to climb the steep staircase to her flat. The very crowded little flat. Surveying the latest additions with a rather jaundiced eye, obviously overspill from her father's

workshop, she dumped her bag on the nearest surface.
Kicking off her shoes, she padded into the bathroom.

Her shoulders slumping tiredly, her lovely eyes
bleak, she turned on the taps, put in a couple of drops
of bath-oil, shut the bathroom door, and stripped off.

Lying in the warm, scented water, she gave a long,
despairing sigh. Why had he come? Why? She didn't
want him here messing up her life.

You're in love with him.

No, I'm not.

Yes, you are, Jenna. You've probably been in love
with him for weeks.

I haven't *known* him for weeks!

Screwing her eyes tight shut to stop the tears, she
fought to get herself under control. Why, oh, why did
he have to come? Why, in fact, *had* he come? To explain about his involvement with Clarissa? Maureen?
Apologise? Well, she didn't care what his feelings
were; she had enough trouble with her own.

She'd looked at it all ways on the long drive home—
backwards, forwards, upside-down—and was still no
nearer discovering why she felt as she did about him.
Or how she could have allowed him such licence in
her villa—and responded. No, she mentally denied
wearily, not only responded, but initiated some of the
lovemaking.

Maybe it *was* just the trauma of the accident,
David's desertion, that had weakened her, made her
vulnerable, open to Bay's particular brand of charm.
Maybe when she was better she wouldn't feel like this
at all. Surely you didn't have to feel something if you
didn't *want* to? And she didn't *want* to, because it
wasn't returned. Lying here examining it all over again
was futile. It wouldn't make it different, no matter

how much she might want it to be. Neither would it take away the pain. Only time could do that. She'd gone out to Spain hurting from David's behaviour and come home hurting from Bay's. So what did that make her? A fool, that was what it made her.

Dragging herself out of the rapidly cooling water, she dried herself, then shrugged into her old towelling dressing-gown. A nice cup of tea, a sleep, and everything would look clearer. She wished she believed that.

Wandering out to the lounge, slightly flushed, escaping tendrils of hair slightly damp, she halted. Her mother hadn't got rid of him. Had she really expected anything else? Her mother was a woman. He was very good with women.

He was examining the books on her shelf; as soon as he became aware of her, he turned his head and gave her a quizzical look.

'I don't want you here!' she exclaimed despairingly.

'Don't you? Tea's just brewing,' he added absently as he returned the book to the shelf. 'I'll go and pour it out.' Without looking at her again, he threaded his way carefully between the motley collection of furniture and went into the kitchen.

And just why was he so po-faced? Because he felt guilty? And if she could just keep from *thinking*, keep her mind perfectly blank, maybe she would be all right. Maybe. Collapsing tiredly on to the old sofa, she put her feet up on an antique footstool; when he returned carrying the tea, he halted in the kitchen doorway to watch her.

'You're a confounded nuisance, Jenna Draycott,' he observed quietly.

'Am I?'

'Yes. And you lied to me.'

'Did I?' she asked in the same uninterested tone.

'Yes. You told me you didn't work.'

Flicking her eyes towards him, then away again, she denied stonily, 'No, I didn't. *You* said I didn't work.'

'But you didn't deny it, did you?'

'Does it matter?'

'No-o, or only insofar as I'm curious to know why you wanted to give me an impression that was clearly false.'

With a little shrug, she took the cup he held out. 'And that's why you came, is it? To find out why I gave a false impression?'

'No.'

'Then why did you come?' she asked defiantly. 'To apologise?'

He looked slightly startled, then shook his head. 'No. I came over to see my publishers,' he explained quietly as he sat in the armchair opposite.

'In Shepton Mallet? I didn't know we had any.'

'You don't. And stop being so bloody difficult,' he reproved, really quite mildly. 'I came to make sure you were all right—and to ask why you told Clarissa about what happened.'

Snapping her head up, she demanded in astonishment, 'Why I what? Well, if that doesn't take the biscuit! *I* tell her?'

'Yes. She was extremely embarrassed.'

'Oh, I'm so sorry!' she retorted sarcastically. 'Poor Clarissa. And if you were so damned concerned about her feelings, you should never have...' Her mouth tight, she demanded, 'Who said I told her?'

'She did.'

'Did she now?' she queried disgustedly. 'To what purpose, I wonder?'

'To no purpose.' With a heavy sigh, he continued, 'Look, I didn't come to row with you, merely to make sure you were all right.'

'Well, I am all right so you can go away.'

'Are you?'

'Yes.'

'And you didn't expect to see me again?'

'No, I *didn't* expect to see you again! Why on earth should I?'

'That's what I'm trying to find out.'

Extremely puzzled, not to say exasperated by this ridiculous exchange, she prompted acidly, 'Because?'

'Because I don't like being manipulated.'

'Oh, good grief! Look, will you just put it into plain English? I'm not very good with enigmas!'

'Very well. Clarissa said that you boasted about how I would follow you to England,' he said bluntly. 'She was worried that I'd be unable to finish the book.'

'Was she, by Jove? Not worried that you were leaving her in the lurch?'

'What?' he asked blankly. 'Now what the hell are you talking about?'

'Clarissa! Your involvement with her!'

'I don't *have* an involvement with her! She's my research assistant! That's all she is! Why in God's name would you think anything else?'

'Because—well, because... Then if you don't have an involvement with her, why didn't you want her to find us together?'

'Because I thought you'd be embarrassed!'

'Pull the other one. Sybarites don't get embarrassed!'

'Jenna . . .' he warned softly.

'Then why did she tell you I told her? If that wasn't the spite of a wronged woman, what was it?'

'Concern!' he said in exasperation.

'Oh, concern, is it? Just walked up to you, did she? And said—what? That I'd told her we'd been romping on the bed? That I was leaving and that I expected you to follow me to England?'

'Don't be ridiculous! You make it sound as though she's some sort of mischief-maker! She was concerned for me, that's all.'

'Because it's happened before?' she asked sweetly, to hide her anger and confusion. 'With Maureen?'

'No, it has not happened before! And I do wish you'd leave Maureen out of every conversation!'

'*I* leave her out?' she exclaimed in disbelief. 'I?'

'All right, all right,' he conceded irritably. 'I merely meant that people—women—are sometimes opportunist. God knows why!'

'God knows why?' she repeated incredulously. 'You really expect me to be fooled by that piece of flummery when you regularly chat up every bimbo on the complex?'

Staring at her as though she'd gone completely round the bend, he demanded blankly, 'When I what?'

Deciding that she'd been monstrously unfair to her own sex, she substituted, ' "Flirting with all the pretty girls" was the actual statement, I believe.'

'*Whose* actual statement?'

'Clarissa's!' she snapped impatiently, and had the satisfaction of seeing his face darken. So far he'd had it all his own arrogant way, but not any more! Jenna might fancy him like crazy, might even be in love with

him, but right at this moment she didn't like him very
much.

His mouth tight, he enunciated precisely, 'Clarissa
does not go around making statements like that. She
might, I will admit, behave like a tiger with one cub
at times, but then, she's paid to protect my interests,
paid to keep people I don't want to see away from
me when I'm working. And she takes her job very
seriously. OK, maybe she treads on some toes, maybe
tact is not her strong point, but then, she's not very
worldly—and don't bloody snort!'

'What do you expect me to do—applaud? Well, go
on; I find this absolutely riveting. How did it all come
about?'

'The parcel.'

'*What* parcel?'

With monumental patience, he explained, 'You gave
her a parcel to give to me, containing my recorder,
which had obviously fallen out of my shorts...'

'No, I didn't,' she denied frostily. 'I gave it to the
maid to give you.'

'And she said,' he resumed determinedly, 'that when
she asked if you needed a hand to pack up your things
and bring them to my villa you told her it wasn't
necessary because you were going back to England to
wait for me there!'

'Oh, really? How very clever. Half fact, half fiction.
And did she apologise?' she asked interestedly.

'What?' he demanded blankly.

'Say it was probably her fault?' A look of disgust
on her lovely face, she put down her cup and got to
her feet. 'Well, you may rest assured that I did not
expect you to follow me; that I do not want you here!
I have no desire to pursue you either for your un-

doubted wealth, position, or your body! And, while we are on the subject, neither do I have any desire to corrupt your brother!'

'Have you finished?' he asked tightly.

'Yes!'

'Good.' Glaring at her, he suddenly frowned. 'Is that true?'

'Yes!'

'Then if she—lied, or got it wrong, I apologise.'

'Thank you.'

Much to her surprise, he gave an unexpectedly rueful smile. 'Go and get dressed. I've booked a table at the Country House Hotel round the corner. We'll discuss it further over lunch.'

'I don't want to discuss it further over lunch!'

'Yes, you do,' he argued with a confusing return to amiability.

'No, I don't!' she exploded. 'You can't just accuse me of all these things and then invite me out to lunch!'

'Of course I can,' he argued with a faint smile. 'I'm starving.'

Staring at him, feeling suddenly helpless and out-flanked, she told him weakly, 'You can't. Oh, why are you doing this?'

'Because I like things clear-cut. Because I like to know the truth.'

'Then you believe me?' she asked in surprise.

'Of course. If you say you aren't pursuing me, then of course I believe you. Clarissa obviously misunderstood. She's sometimes a bit paranoid about my privacy.'

'Paranoid? The woman's positively out of her tree—or extraordinarily clever. All those half-sentences . . . innuendoes . . . blaming herself——'

'Jenna,' he interrupted, 'go and get dressed. We can discuss it over lunch.'

'I don't want to discuss it. I want you to go away.'

'Which I will, if that's what you really want, when we've had lunch.'

'It is what I want,' she said defiantly. And she should have left it there, she knew that she should, but some demon made her ask, 'And if it wasn't what I wanted? If I wanted you to stay?'

His eyes narrowed slightly, and the drawl was suddenly back. Getting lazily to his feet, he walked to stand in front of her. Tilting her chin up with one finger, a finger that seemed to burn her skin, he said slowly, 'I like you, Jenna. I'm not entirely sure I understand you, but I do like you—very much. No, more than very much—and, I have to confess, against my will—but if you are asking for some sort of commitment there won't be one. I never gave you reason to believe otherwise, did I?'

'No,' she admitted tightly.

'No, because I never do.'

'Why?' she asked, surprised by the admission. 'What about if you fall in love with someone?'

'Love? A very transient emotion in my experience. But if I did? No, not even then. Anyway, there can be no permanent involvement until Mark's grown-up and no longer needs me.'

'You don't think he needs a mother?' she couldn't resist taunting. Stepping back, she deliberately broke the contact between them because it was becoming unbearable to have him so close.

'No, Jenna, I don't think he needs a mother. Any feminine influence he might need is provided for at the moment by——'

'Clarissa—yes, I know.'

'Good. So go and get ready.'

And because he didn't look as though he would go away, because it might be easier to deal with him when there were other people around, she went to do so.

'It's not too far for you?' he asked casually as they walked round to the hotel.

'No,' she denied in surprise; oddly enough, she hadn't given her leg a thought since he'd arrived. And what did that mean? she wondered drearily. That he was a cure of ailments?

When they walked into the hotel, Jenna was greeted by the owner like a long-lost daughter. 'Jenna! Better now?'

'Much.'

'Splendid. Come on through; you have the dining-room to yourselves.'

'Oh, Jim!' she exclaimed worriedly. 'Are things that bad?'

''Fraid so,' he admitted, 'but not to worry. Maggie is positively yearning to try out some new dishes on you.'

With a laugh that sounded hollow even to herself, she said softly, 'So make sure we order them?'

'No need to order them—you get them whether you like it or not!' He did, however, let them choose where to sit.

'By the window, please,' Jenna requested.

He seated them, gave Bay a blatant once-over, nodded, and went off to fetch the wine-list.

'Maggie is his wife,' Jenna explained, needing to say something. 'The best cook in the whole wide world.'

He merely smiled. 'Business is slow, I take it?'

With a little sigh, she nodded. 'For us all. Not so many tourists this year. We're all desperately trying to hang on and hope things pick up.'

'You've always lived here?'

'Mmm. I spent a couple of years in London learning my trade, so to speak, and couldn't wait to get back. Bristol, Frome, Bath, Glastonbury all in spitting distance, nice, friendly people . . .'

'And you like to feel comfortable? Need to know people?'

'Yes.' And if that made her sound suburban she didn't care. 'I like my chums around me, need the comfort of being——'

'Liked?'

'Sounds conceited, but yes. I like to see new places, meet strangers, have new conversations, but I like to come home. I don't like confrontations, arguments. I can cope with dramas, crises, but not malicious behaviour, not—nastiness. It upsets me.' Shut up, Jenna, she told herself; he can't be even remotely interested. But Mark had been right, hadn't he? You did find yourself telling him things. Thankfully, they were interrupted by Jim with the wine-list. Bay took it with a smile, glanced swiftly through it, and ordered. Jim looked approving. Not that she cared, but Bay obviously knew about wine. Jim absolutely hated it when people pretended to be experts and only proved themselves woefully ignorant. Much better to be honest and ask his advice.

While the wine was opened, tasted, approved, Jenna gazed out into the garden. A blackbird was sunning itself on the path, wings spread; a squirrel leapt up on to the bird-table, looked disapproving at what was on offer and scampered away. She wished she could.

He might not be involved with Clarissa, but he didn't want any sort of commitment either. Back to square one. And being with him was hell, because she kept seeing him naked, pictures in her head of how it had been on her bed.

'Tell me about you,' he requested softly, breaking into her reverie.

Glancing at him, then lowering her eyes to the cloth, she murmured, 'Not much to tell.'

'Then tell me about the drive home.'

Her mother *had* been busy. And because this was all so silly, because she didn't really know what to say, Jenna resorted to flippancy. 'It was long.'

'Figures. Your nose looks better.'

'Yes.'

'Scabbing nicely. I like your mother.'

'So do I. Was she reclining?'

He gave a wide smile, then chuckled. 'Yes, she was. And she said that if your father doesn't *immediately* notice she's a sybarite she'll ask for a divorce.'

Her smile mechanical, she looked down again. I don't want to be here, she thought, making polite conversation. She wanted it to be tomorrow, or next week, but they couldn't sit there in silence, so an effort had to be made. She would never have guessed that she was such a damned good actress. And she felt sick. 'Did you fly over?'

'Mmm. You'd have been proud of me. There were no flights available, all seats fully booked, so I became extremely prima donnaish, insisted on preferential treatment, and shamelessly and without a qualm forced a very old lady——'

'With young child.'

'With young child,' he agreed, 'naturally, possibly even a sick and ailing young child, to give up her seat to me.'

'And here you are.'

'Yes. Here I am.'

'How?'

He blinked and queried comically, 'How?'

'Yes. As in how did you manage to get hold of Helen, who you informed me you did not know...? I assume that is how you found me?'

'Yes. All done with unbelievable ease. I merely asked one of the secretarys in the management office on the complex if she could give me Helen's phone number...'

'Which she obviously did, despite the fact that they aren't supposed to do so.'

'No.'

'But then, you're rich and famous...'

'Stop it,' he ordered gently. He reached out as if to touch her, then changed his mind. With a little sigh, he continued, 'She told me about the accident, about what you did...'

A quiver of irritation crossed her face, and she asked with a trace of bitterness, 'Is that why you came? Because heroines deserve better treatment?'

'No. I came to make sure you were all right—and to find out about the real Jenna.'

'In case Clarissa hadn't been telling the truth?' she couldn't resist asking.

'No—in case there were mitigating circumstances. And it was never meant——' Breaking off, he pulled a face, then leaned back in his chair. Staring at her, he said quietly, 'When I first met you, I was surprised because I felt an immediate tug of attraction. Then I

persuaded myself that it was a case of easy on the
mind, easy on the eye. And when I saw you again in
the bar later you amused and intrigued me. You were
different, and I liked you.'

'An amusing companion,' she put in quietly.

'Yes. And so when Mark asked if you could come
to Albacete I agreed, because I thought you would be
good company, and because when I'm driving I like
having someone to talk to. Mark knew that, and because he liked you he wanted me to.'

'Because I was gentle and sweet.'

'Don't be waspish,' he reproved. 'And possibly
that's all it would ever have been, only you left your
bag in the restaurant, and—things changed. And then
you changed. Suddenly, you were different. More—
brittle. Why, Jenna? Because you really had come to
get your bag?'

Staring at him, almost having forgotten that she'd
never explained why she'd needed it, she shrugged.
'It contained my pain-killers.'

'I see. And Cannes? Monte Carlo? Have you ever
been there?'

With a funny little smile, she shook her head. 'No.'

'But you let me believe it. Let me believe you selfish
when you wouldn't, as I thought, help to look for
Mark. Why?'

'How is Mark?'

'Oh, Jenna...' Searching her lovely face, he gave
up trying to force confidences. 'He's fine. Fully re-
covered from his fright.' His eyes darkening momen-
tarily, he added, 'And if he hadn't managed to get
out of that mine, we might never have found him.'

'No,' she agreed seriously, 'and that might have
been something you could genuinely have levelled at

me. I think it was my fault. It was me who told him about them.'

'No. If not you, it would have been someone else.'

'Maybe. Did you tell him off?' she asked curiously as she remembered what Clarissa had said.

'Tell him off?' he echoed in surprise. 'Why on earth would I do that? It was an accident, and you can't keep thirteen-year-old boys from having *those*. Did you think I should have done?'

'No, I think you should have given him a hug.'

'I did.' A gentle smile in his eyes that threatened to be her undoing, he asked, 'Was there someone to give you one? Make you feel better when you had your accident?'

'Yes. The fireman who cut me out. He gave me a hug.' And in reaction and shock she had cried all over the front of his uniform.

'I'm glad. And Helen's grandson? The little boy you saved? Is he all better now?'

'Yes, he's all better now.'

'Good. I remember reading about it at the time, but the newspapers didn't give your name. Because you didn't want them to?'

'Yes.'

They broke off when Jim came to remove their soup plates, and bring them their main meal, then he asked idly, 'What's your father like?'

'Dad? He's a darling.'

'And he restores the furniture your mother sells?'

'Yes, although I have to admit not all of it finds its way into the shop. Some pieces he simply can't bear to part with. The house is crammed with "special cases".'

'As is your flat! And is that where you got your passion from?'

'Yes. From as far back as I can remember, I used to accompany him on expeditions to junk shops, antique shops, markets. We could never afford to buy anything really worthwhile, but we liked to dream. He's nice, my Dad.' Toying with asparagus tips that she didn't really want, she asked curiously, 'What were your parents like?'

'Wealthy.'

Somewhat startled by the bitter note in his voice, she looked at him. He was watching her with a rather satirical gleam in his eyes. 'There must be more than that.'

'Must there? Why?'

'Because there must! *They* must have had feelings! *You* must have had feelings about them: love, affection, something! And when they died so tragically... There has to have been something more than wealth.'

'Nannies?' he offered with dry sarcasm.

'Oh. That's sad. And is that why you said you'd seen firsthand what wealth could do to young minds? Because of what it did to you?'

'No.' Still staring at her, he wasn't going to elaborate, she thought, but then he sighed, gave an odd little shrug. 'Not to me, to my sister. Althea.'

'Pretty name,' she commented inadequately.

'Yes. She was a pretty girl.'

'Was?'

'Yes. Was. Seventeen years old, and she threw it all away. Bright, pretty, spoilt, selfish, and she thought she could have it all.' A rather distant look in his eyes, he sighed again. 'I was away at boarding-school, didn't know about her reckless lifestyle until it was too late. And even if I had I doubt it would have made any difference. She was on a roller-coaster ride to hell—and didn't want to get off. She thought it exciting, glamorous, and I was just the stuffy elder brother.'

'How did she die?' she asked quietly.

'Drugs, drink, the usual tragic story. . .'

'And your parents didn't try to stop her?'

'Of course they tried to stop her!' he exclaimed almost angrily. 'But by the time they actually admitted she had a problem, that they'd been wrong to give her whatever she wanted—money, possessions— as an expression of their love, it was too late! Maybe having Mark was an attempt by my parents at getting it right; I don't know. There was a lot of anger and bitterness after Althea died. Everyone blaming everyone else. I felt—impotent. And guilty, because I had never liked her very much.'

'And so, when they died, you determined to do better by Mark.'

'Yes, at least to give him *time*. A decent set of values.'

'Yes.' She'd been incredibly lucky in her upbringing, but at least she understood in part the reason for Bay's behaviour in Spain. Understood his protectiveness towards his young brother.

When Jim came to remove their plates, she gave him a little glance of apology for not having done the excellent meal justice. 'I wasn't very hungry,' she excused herself inadequately.

'Never mind. What about some strawberry gateau? No? Coffee?'

'No, thank you.' When Bay also shook his head, she added, 'Will you thank Maggie for the meal? And apologise?'

'Why not go and thank her yourself?' Bay asked, and looked surprised when Jim laughed.

'She gets embarrassed,' Jenna explained. 'She's painfully shy. Hates to be made a fuss of.'

'A bit like you, in fact.'

'*I'm* not painfully shy,' she denied.

'No, but you don't like to be made a fuss of— No,' he qualified, 'you don't like a fuss to be made of what you *do*.'

'No more do you.'

'No. Ready?'

With a little nod, she got to her feet. Was that to be it? Would he go now? And would she never see him again? Despite the fact that he'd found her attractive? It hurt. There was a tight pain inside, an awful ache in her heart, in her throat. She thought she might be in love with him; like to spend the rest of her life with him. Blinking away the prickling in her eyes, she led the way out.

When they reached the corner, she halted in dismay as she saw the mother of one of her dance pupils come out of the butchers. Damn. Perhaps she wouldn't see her...

'Are you all right?' Bay asked in concern.

'What? Oh, yes, I just...' With a long sigh, she pinned a bright smile on her face as Mrs West advanced towards them.

'Jenna!' she exclaimed. 'How are you? How was Spain?'

'Fine, I——'

'And even more to the point, when are you coming back? Anita is very good, of course she's very good, but she isn't *you*. So when might we look for you?'

'Not for a few weeks yet, I'm afraid, although I will be coming in to keep a watching brief, so to speak.'

'Good, good. Now don't think me rude, but I'm in the most frightful hurry. Must dash; nice to have seen you.' Her smile wide, she hurried on.

'Who on earth,' Bay questioned, 'was that?'

'Mrs West.'

Turning a very humorous look on her, he prompted, 'Who is?'

With supreme reluctance, she admitted, 'The mother of one of my students.'

'Currently being seen to by Anita,' he nodded, 'who is very good, but is not you. Students of what?' he demanded.

'Dance,' she muttered.

'Dance?' he exclaimed in astonishment. 'You're a dance teacher?'

'Yes,' she admitted grudgingly. 'Tap, ballet...'

'Tap?' he asked in apparent delight. 'Shuffle, hop, step?'

With a reluctant smile, she nodded, then glanced up at him. In his expression she saw the dawning knowledge of what injuring her leg must have meant to her, saw sympathy, understanding, and looked quickly away.

'I don't know you at all, do I?' he mused quietly.

'No.' Not wanting to talk about it, discuss it, receive expressions of sympathy, she urged him into motion, smiled vaguely at a young police constable, then halted in surprise when he caught her arm.

'Not that way, love; there's been an accident. Where do you need to go?'

'Makim Street.'

'Then cut through the supermarket car park, can you?'

'Yes, of course.' Swallowing the nausea that rose unbidden, she managed to ask, 'Was it a bad accident?'

'No, just some idiot took the corner too fast and went into the wall. But there's glass everywhere and we need the road clear so that the tow-truck and the ambulance can get through.'

Nodding, not wanting to know any further details, because if there was an ambulance, then someone had been injured, she automatically redirected Bay to the narrow alley on their right. Taking a deep breath, she held it for a moment, then slowly let it out, thankful that the moment of dizziness had passed. She didn't think Bay had noticed anything and was startled when he stopped her, turned her so that he could look down into her face.

'Are you all right?'

'Yes. I'm fine,' she said determinedly.

Taking her hand, he gave it a comforting squeeze. 'Did you have counselling?' he asked. 'For accident trauma?'

'No.'

'Did they offer it?'

She shook her head. 'Even if they had, I'm not sure I would have gone. I know myself well enough to know that I'm best left to sort things out on my own. It doesn't trouble me often,' she lied. 'Just sometimes little things remind me and bring it all back.'

'Like seeing coaches?'

'No, funnily enough, that doesn't bother me at all, even ones that are the same make, colour, et cetera as the one that was in the crash. Nor the sight of blood.' With a funny little grimace, she added, 'You'll really laugh, but do you know what set it off last time? A tin of sardines.'

He didn't laugh, just released her hand and hugged her warmly to his side. 'I never did like sardines. Nasty greasy little things.'

With a half-hearted smile, she began to move on. And soon he would be gone... She didn't want him to go. A few more yards and the stupid little episode would be over.

When they reached the shop there was a car parked outside, and because she didn't want to think about him going, was trying so very hard to hold herself together, Jenna latched on to incidentals. 'She'll get a parking ticket if she's not careful,' she murmured.

His arm dropped from her shoulders, and she became aware of his unnatural stillness. Turning to look up at him, she found him staring at the car, and a slow, derisive smile twisted his mouth as a woman climbed from behind the wheel and slowly turned to face them.

'Bay? Is something wrong?'

'Wrong? Now what on earth could be wrong?' he drawled in the way that she hated as he continued to watch the woman.

'I don't know; that's why I asked. Do you know her?'

'Of course I know her. Don't you?'

'Me?' she asked in surprise. 'No, why would I know her?'

'Just a passing thought.' Catching her arm, he led her across the road. 'Allow me to introduce you—to my wife.'

CHAPTER NINE

'YOUR wife?' Jenna echoed blankly. 'You have a wife? What on earth is *she* doing here?' Then, recalling how stupid she was being, but somehow unable to unscramble her brain, she asked even more stupidly, 'Is she meeting you? Did she *know* you would be here?'

'That, my dear Jenna, is most definitely the question,' he drawled with a sideways glance.

'Well, don't look at me!' she retorted, a horrible little sick feeling inside of her. '*I* didn't tell her! I didn't even know you were married!'

'Was, Jenna. Was.'

'Was?' she echoed just as stupidly.

'Mmm. Past tense.'

'Oh.' Staring at the woman as they slowly approached her, she asked feebly, 'Does she *often* follow you around?'

He gave a bitter laugh, but didn't answer. 'Maureen,' he greeted her derisively.

Maureen? Maureen was his ex-wife? A woman he had once been married to? She didn't know why it astonished her so much, but it did. And both Clarissa and Bay had intimated that she was like her. And she wasn't. She wasn't like her at all! Maureen was taller, slimmer, her hair was brown, her *eyes* were brown!

With a thoroughly malicious smile on her face, Maureen handed him a folded magazine. 'I did warn you, didn't I?' she taunted softly. 'You should know by now that I *always* do as I promise. I think you'll find page thirty-two absolutely riveting, darling,' she purred. Turning to a bewildered Jenna, she gave her a saccharine smile. 'Hello, Jenna, how very nice to see you again.' Climbing back into her car, she drove away.

'Why did she say that? And how does she know who I am?' Jenna demanded numbly as she continued to stare after the little red car. 'I've never seen her before in my life.'

'Haven't you?' His mouth twisting, he leaned against the wall beside the shop and opened the magazine.

'No. And why did she say all those things?'

'Revenge.'

'Revenge for what?' Turning to look at him, she felt an overwhelming desire to hit him when he only glanced up, one eyebrow raised. 'What are you looking at me like that for? You think I know why she wants revenge?' Was he late with maintenance payments? she wondered almost hysterically. But you only paid maintenance if there were children, didn't you? Did he *have* children? Quite possibly. He could have a dozen for all she knew! And he looked so— unconcerned as he leaned against the wall idly turning pages. Casually dressed, yet somehow elegant even in jeans and a blue shirt; powerful... She wanted to know what on earth was going on. Wanted to snatch the magazine out of his hand and look at page thirty two! And how on earth were you ever supposed to know what he was thinking, feeling, when he wore that damned *nothing* expression?

'Ah!' he exclaimed softly.

' "Ah" what?' she demanded.

Lowering the magazine, he stared at her, his face expressionless. 'My, my, my, you have been a busy little girl, haven't you?'

'What?'

'And I so very nearly believed you, didn't I?'

'Believed what?'

'And you'd *really* think I'd learn, wouldn't you?' he asked softly, but with such menace that she took a step backwards. 'You really would think I would.' Crumpling the magazine he thrust it at her. 'What a superb actress you are, Jenna. Really worthy of an Oscar! You sat in that damned hotel, shy, inarticulate, *believable*, and all the time... Dear God, but you're good.'

'What? Stop it! Stop it! I don't know what you're talking about! And I'm not shy,' she said stupidly.

'No, because, of course, it wasn't shyness, was it? You were being deliberately obtuse. Refusing to answer questions... Where did you meet her? Albacete? While I was doing research? That would, of course, explain why you changed, became brittle— because you were afraid I would find out. If I hadn't thrown you out of my room, would she have burst in wielding a camera?'

'No! I've never *met* her!'

'Haven't you? Then how did you know about her? You never did explain that.'

'I *didn't* know about her! Clarissa mentioned her— she did!' she insisted fiercely in the face of his disbelief. 'Told me I was like her—and not to mention her to you! Dear God,' she burst out, 'I would dearly love to know what makes you so suspicious!'

'Life,' he said succinctly. 'And of *course* you didn't want me to come here. No wonder you were nervous.

How much did she pay you? Enough for another holiday in the sun?' With a look of disgust, he walked away. No, not only disgust, she thought in disordered bewilderment, hurt—as though he was hurt, disillusioned.

Staring after him, even after he'd turned the corner, she only came to herself when her mother opened the shop door. 'Now what little drama are we enacting?' she asked in amusement.

'What?' Turning towards her, her face still blank, Jenna weakly shook her head. 'I don't know. He just walked off!'

'And without his magazine?'

'What?' Her face still screwed up in frowning confusion, she glanced down at the magazine. It was still folded to page thirty-two and as she glanced down the columns, stared at the pictures, her confusion gave way to astonishment, then understanding, and then anger. 'He really *did* believe it was me!'

'You who what?' her mother asked interestedly.

'Told her! His wife!'

'He's married?' she exclaimed. 'Oh, the rat! Oh, hello, Dora,' she added all in the same breath as she smiled warmly at the lady from the shop next door. 'Son all right? Good, good.' Catching hold of her daughter's arm, she drew her inside the shop and firmly closed the door. 'Was that his wife I saw outside on the pavement?'

'Yes,' Jenna muttered as she continued to scan the article. 'Well, ex-wife anyway.'

'Ah, that's better.'

'No, it isn't!' Jenna denied. 'This is awful!' she exclaimed weakly. 'It says he threw his wife out. Refused to acknowledge her... And then it says... Oh,

I don't believe that! Oh, and that's not true ... It implies that I——'

'Jenna!' her mother interrupted in exasperation. '*Tell* me! Lucidly!'

Glancing up, her eyes unfocused, she asked, 'Did he really believe I would do that?'

'I don't know, darling; I don't know what you're talking about!' Twitching the magazine out of Jenna's lax hold, she frowned down at it. 'Oh, well, really!' she exclaimed. 'Threw his wife out and then refused to support her? Who wrote this rubbish? Humiliated her? What rot!'

'No,' Jenna denied faintly, 'he might have done that. He can be a bit ... But why imply that *I* gave out all this information? I mean, how on earth would I know what he earned for his last book? How would I know about his——?'

'Affairs?' her mother asked absently as she continued to read. 'Oh.' Looking up, staring at her daughter over the lowered magazine, she asked almost hesitantly, 'Were you ...? I mean, did ...? Only it says ...'

'What does it say?' Jenna asked slowly, a dawning expression of horror on her face. She'd only got halfway down the second column. But whoever had written the article had obviously been at the complex—or at least had inside information, detailed inside information. Surely they hadn't put in anything *personal*? Taking the magazine, she had to force herself to actually read it. 'Oh, my God,' she said weakly.

'It doesn't actually *name* you,' his mother comforted. 'And it doesn't actually categorically state that you were—er—lovers ...'

'It doesn't have to, does it?' she asked bitterly. 'They've described me well enough! And I did not bloody seduce him!'

'No, dear.'

'I didn't! But how did they know all about Albacete? The way it's crafted, it implies that I inveigled my way into his affections in order to *expose* him! Why?' she wondered aloud in bewilderment. 'For what possible reason? It's so—malicious!'

'Yes, it is. Someone doesn't like you very much, Jenna—and likes Bay even less!'

'His wife,' she murmured. 'He seemed to think she was here out of revenge.'

'And she promoted the article, do you think?'

'I don't know. But if she did, then someone must have told her what went on in Spain, because I didn't actually see *her* there, and *someone* must have been in Albacete!' Her eyes widening, she murmured, 'Clarissa.'

'Who's Clarissa?'

'Bay's research assistant,' she explained in the same distracted voice.

'Ah. Well, she's certainly lived up to her job description, hasn't she?'

'It isn't funny,' she reproved weakly.

'No, Jenna, it isn't.'

'But why? I barely knew the girl—and Bay assured me there wasn't anything between them. Even if there was, there hasn't been time for her to write this *and* get it published since I left Spai—— No, no, wait a minute,' she murmured, with a frown. 'Clarissa couldn't have been in Albacete—at least, I didn't see her, but . . . The man in Reception,' she whispered, as she suddenly remembered the little incident when she'd returned from the wash-room. 'I *bet* that's who it was: a reporter. He must have been *following* us. But at whose instigation? Clarissa or Maureen?'

'Sounds a bit paranoid, don't you think?' her mother asked hesitantly. 'I mean, being followed.'

'No. In fact, I'd lay money on it! And he must have seen me go into Bay's room ... Oh, Mother, what am I going to do?' she wailed.

'What can you do, except ignore it?'

'But he thought *I* did it!'

'Then he's a fool. Er, did you go into his room?' she asked interestedly.

'Yes.' Glancing up, seeing her mother's expression, Jenna gave her a look of disgust. 'I went to get my pain-killers,' she reproved with quiet dignity.

'Ah.' Then she smiled, gently. 'Oh, darling, did you like him so very much?'

'Yes.'

'In love with him?'

'I don't know,' she muttered defeatedly. 'But I did *like* him!' With a bitter laugh, she commented, 'I'm not very lucky in the romance stakes, am I? First David, now Bay. Not that Bay ever professed to love me. In fact, he made it very clear that he wanted no commitment ... Anyway, even if he had, our life-styles are poles apart. He hob-nobs with the rich and famous as though they were ordinary!'

'They are ordinary,' her mother pointed out softly. 'Inside I expect they are very ordinary, and it's not like you to be overwhelmed by status.'

'I'm not overwhelmed,' she denied, 'just—disappointed, I guess. Nobody ever seems to turn out as I expect, do they? But to think that I had a hand in this—gutter rubbish ...'

'He'll find out the truth.'

'No, he won't. Why should he? And even if he does ...' Glancing down at the magazine, she tossed it distastefully on to a nearby cabinet. '*And* she pretended we knew each other.'

'Who? Clarissa?'

'*No*, Maureen!'

'Oh.'

With a long sigh, she asked listlessly, 'Did you know? When you first met Daddy?'

'Oh, yes,' she admitted softly.

'Immediately?' Jenna demanded, as though it weren't somehow allowed.

'Mmm-hmm.'

'How old were you?'

'Twenty-eight.'

'That was old, wasn't it? Then?'

'Jenna! I'm only fifty-four. You don't need to make it sound as though it was in the last century!'

'Sorry,' she apologised with a slight smile. 'But it was, wasn't it?'

'Mmm, all the old cats gleefully pronouncing me to be on the shelf.'

'And they did think it funny when you married Dad? I mean, you were very pretty...'

'I'm still very pretty!'

'Mmm, modest too,' her daughter teased, but her heart wasn't really in it. 'But Daddy wasn't exactly an Adonis, was he?'

'No,' her mother conceded with a fond smile. 'Not an Adonis. Shorter than me, going bald, getting a tummy on him, and I love him so much, Jenna, you wouldn't believe.'

'Yes, I would, I——'

'Although I do hope,' her mother continued stringently, 'that you aren't foolish enough to equate good looks with good breeding and——'

'No,' she sighed, 'it's just that people—not me,' she emphasised, 'but people expect someone pretty to marry a handsome prince, don't they?'

'Possibly.'

'Not that I want a handsome prince,' she asserted quietly. 'I just want, wish——'

'For the same as me?'

'Yes. Someone to look at me the way Daddy looks at you. Someone who will adore the very ground I walk on. Someone I can adore in return. Someone who doesn't think I'm something I'm not. Is that asking too much?'

'*I* don't think so. But then, I have been so incredibly lucky.'

'Yes. Do you think it's rebound stuff? I didn't want to feel like this about him, you know, because I could see it wouldn't go anywhere. It just happened. Just the thought of him made me want to smile——' Breaking off, she hastily swallowed. 'Oh, well, no use crying about it, is there? I think I'll go up and have a sleep. I'm tired.' Giving her mother a distracted smile, she hurried up to her flat and thankfully closed the door—and finally allowed the tears to fall.

There was a hope, a small hope, that he would discover the truth—phone, write, come to see her again. But, as the weeks passed, as September slipped into October, she was forced to admit the truth. He was not coming back. So get on with your life, Jenna, she told herself. The pain in her leg gradually lessened and, although it would still be some time before she could dance again, run, her life slowly returned to

normal. Only her emotions remained in constant up-
heaval. She would catch herself gazing wistfully into
the distance, and it took a supreme effort to shove
him back into the recesses of her mind, only to find
moments later that he was intruding once again. Books
reminded her of him, sunshine reminded her of him,
and she only had to gaze at the scar on her knee, see
a yukka plant, and it would all flood back.

How long would it take, she sometimes wondered
in despair, before another relationship was possible?
At the moment, it felt like forever. It hadn't felt like
this with David. Obviously she hadn't loved David,
only thought she had. Her sighs seemed to get longer,
deeper.

Kneeling on the floor in the little workshop, stripping
varnish from an old chair, she heard the shop door
ping, and reluctantly got to her feet. Her parents were
off at an auction in Bristol, and ignoring a potential
customer in this economic climate wasn't even to be
thought of. As she wiped her hands on an old rag,
her smile of welcome faded and died. Reality seemed
suspended, time stopped, and she found herself unable
to move, unable to speak, unable to do anything but
stare.

He leaned in the doorway, gave a sardonic smile.
But his eyes didn't smile; they were completely and
utterly serious. He was still brown, his hair needed
cutting, his green shirt was highly unsuitable for a
chilly October day—and such a feeling of love washed
over her that she shut her eyes in despair.

'I've been rehearsing things to say all the way from
the airport,' he said quietly, and his voice was still the

same—deep, sexy, exquisite torture. 'An apology seemed inadequate, insulting.'

Forcing her vocal cords into use, she whispered, 'How long have you known?'

'A few weeks,' he admitted. 'I was going to phone you, then I was going to write...' He sighed, gave an odd smile. 'I thought I could forget you—and I couldn't.'

Deciding that her legs weren't going to support her for very much longer, she sank down on to the *chaise-longue* that her mother had once reclined on. That incident seemed a lifetime ago. She watched him close the door, put the snick up, turn the sign to closed. And even when he walked towards her, sat beside her, his strong forearms along his knees, she couldn't move.

He gently removed the rag from her nerveless fingers and put it on the floor, turned his face towards her, close enough for his warm breath to feather against her mouth. Still she couldn't move, and although she tried very hard to deny feeling any of the things she was feeling, ignore the warm pain in her tummy, she couldn't drag her eyes away from his. He was back, and she didn't know what to do.

His nose was almost touching hers, his lashes a dark fan as he transferred his gaze to her mouth—then he kissed her, oh, so very softly, and Jenna gasped because it was electrifying.

'I tramped the Sierra Nevada and wanted you with me. Old smuggling trails on donkeyback, and I wanted you beside me.'

She wanted to cough, clear the blockage in her throat, uncramp her muscles, do something, anything, and she couldn't. She found her eyes straying

to his mouth, watched his words form, was mesmerised by the shape of his bottom lip, the flash of
white teeth, and the pain spread, curled downwards,
became a shiver.

'Part your mouth,' he urged softly, and such was
her confusion that she did, her heart beating slowly,
unevenly—and still he waited, his eyes on her mouth.
'I want to make love to you,' he whispered. 'I want
to lay you beneath me, tangle my fingers in your glo-
rious hair, and love you.' His lower lip caught hers,
brushed against it; his tongue slid inside, withdrew,
and Jenna arched involuntarily, dragged a breath deep
into her lungs—and the phone rang.

Reaching out an automatic hand, Bay picked it up,
handed it to her, and as she turned her head to speak
into the mouthpiece he touched his tongue to her ear.

Her senses totally disordered, her breathing erratic,
as Bay alternately blew then licked her ear, she barely
listened to the man on the other end of the phone as
he solemnly listed all the pieces of furniture he had
for restoration. She murmured yes and no in hopefully appropriate places, turned without conscious
thought to meet Bay's mouth as it roved across her
cheek, and totally forgot about the man on the other
end of the phone. The receiver was slowly lowered to
lie in her lap, her hand still coiled loosely round the
plastic—deaf, blind, and totally indifferent to the
eager sounds being emitted, she was unable to do
anything but respond to Bay's magnetic assault. Being
laconic gave a whole new meaning to lovemaking.
Unhurried, drowsy almost, it was erotic and moreish,
and she felt totally incapable of refusing any demand
he might make. And as for neck zones, how on earth

had she got through twenty-six years of life without knowing there were so many zones of erotica?

His hands didn't wander; in fact they did absolutely nothing to which she could object—very clever psychology, because she wanted, quite desperately, for him to do the very things he pointedly wasn't doing. At the back of her mind was an insistent little voice saying, No, stop, don't. But her breasts felt heavy, swollen, needing to be cupped. Read my mind. Dear God, read my mind, she pleaded silently—but he didn't. He ignored her silent demands. And if this was heaven, she very badly wanted to fall from grace.

He was warm and solid, and she had needed this so much. Releasing the now silent receiver, she touched one hand to his strong chest, found buttons, and finally his warm flesh. Her head felt too heavy, her neck weak, and through the fringe of her lashes she watched her fingers describe delicious little circles on his smooth body, anticipated the taste of him... A car backfired somewhere outside, and she jerked, stared up at him in shock.

'That wasn't fair,' she whispered shakily.

'No,' he agreed, 'neither was it enough.'

Her eyes widening, she swallowed the constriction in her throat.

'Don't you think we've lied to ourselves long enough? We both knew what we wanted in Albacete, and both have been denying it.'

'You don't want a commitment,' she pointed out, her voice still weak, unsteady.

'No.' Holding her eyes, he waited.

If she insisted it was what she wanted, he would go away again, wouldn't he? And she didn't want him to go away. Although maybe if she got to know him better she wouldn't like him so much. Maybe it would all fizzle out... And if it didn't, well, some people had relationships that lasted years—and then eventually they married. He liked her, wanted her; might it not deepen into something else if she waited, was patient? Wasn't it worth a try? She'd never felt this way before. Wasn't it worth fighting for?

Rising to his feet, he held out one hand, and because she didn't want him to go she put her own into it, allowed him to draw her to her feet. He led the way upstairs, and firmly closed the door to the flat. She felt nervous, disorientated. Don't be silly, Jenna. It's only Bay, she told herself. Yes. Only Bay.

'Sit down,' he ordered softly.

'What?'

He gave a faint smile, but she could feel the tension in him, the desire, almost feel the heat from his skin. 'In the chair.'

On legs that shook, she walked to the armchair and collapsed weakly into it. He followed, parted her knees and knelt between them, and the little flutter in the pit of her stomach became a positive cramp. Warmth spread along her thighs, and she was very aware, as she knew he was, that her nipples had hardened and were pressing softly against her shirt. There was a dryness in her mouth, a constriction in her chest; with a fluttery little sigh, she reached out to push the tangled hair off his forehead. She had not intended her hand to stay, but it seemed extraordinarily difficult to summon up the energy to remove it.

'Napes are nice,' he prompted thickly, and, as her hand moved obediently to his nape, he gave an ecstatic shiver.

It wasn't supposed to be like this, she thought almost despairingly. Weren't you supposed to meet someone and immediately know that he was the one? Like with her mother? No one had ever said it would be hedged about with confusion. There was also a strong desire to have it all taken out of her hands, not to have to think. She gave a long, shuddery sigh.

His eyes had darkened, she saw; then she was unable to see anything as he reached out and slowly began to undo the buttons on her shirt.

She didn't say a word; didn't protest, as she should have done, didn't stop him; didn't even consider doing so; didn't even hate herself for being so weak-willed. When the buttons were all undone, when the soft material had been parted, he touched one finger to the valley between her breasts and she gave an involuntary little gasp. And when he used that same finger to ease her lacy bra to one side, let his eyes linger on his discovery, she stopped breathing altogether.

Leaning forward, unbelievably, tantalisingly, slowly, he touched his tongue to the nipple.

Oh, God.

She hadn't intended for this to happen—at least, she didn't think she had—but now that it was happening her body had its own ideas about what it wanted. And perhaps he was a mind-reader, because he turned his attention to her skirt. Her old navy denim skirt that she wore for dirty jobs in the workshop, the skirt that buttoned up at the front, hem to waistband. His eyes on hers, he began to slip the buttons free.

Only one more button to go... His eyes moved from hers, he touched one finger to the very part of her that was aching so much and her breath exploded outwards. With a little groan, she clutched his wrist.

'No?' he asked thickly as he raised his eyes once more to hers, and she saw the desire in them, the need.

'No...yes... Oh, God, I don't know,' she breathed agitatedly. 'I'm not——'

'Promiscuous? Yes, I know. No,' he added pointedly, 'neither am I.' In one swift motion he stood, scooped her out of the chair and laid her supine on the floor. Joining her, he stared down into her eyes, and then began to kiss her. Long, gentle kisses—capable, assured, teasing her into acquiescence while his long, supple fingers undid the final button on her skirt. He eased it from beneath her, did the same with her shirt, and when she lay in just her bra and pants he lifted his mouth, took a deep breath, and gave her such a blindingly sweet smile that her heart, and all her objections, melted.

'Your turn,' he said, and his beautiful voice sounded ragged, just a little bit rough.

She had tried to persuade herself over the past few agonising weeks that their lovemaking in Spain hadn't been special; that proximity and drama, her own vulnerability, had heightened the incident out of all proportion. Self-deceit was no longer possible. It had been special, and now he taught her things she hadn't known were possible; he guided her own hands with a surety and a delicacy that frightened and delighted her.

'Is that what comes of being a writer?' she whispered shakily when they lay, for the moment, spent.

'Mmm.' He smiled as he happily smoothed her flat stomach with one large palm. 'Research, and a great deal of imagination.'

How many women had he needed in his research to reach that level of perfection?

As if he understood, he pressed a soft kiss to her nose. 'Research can be undertaken equally well by reading.'

With a weak smile, she protested, 'You didn't learn all *that* by reading!'

'How do you know?'

'I don't, of course,' she admitted with a sigh.

'Then you shouldn't make judgements.'

'No.' Unable to help herself, as though someone else had taken over her body, she traced his exquisite mouth with her finger. 'You didn't tell me who gave out the information for that article.'

'Did I need to?' he asked equally softly.

'No. Clarissa?'

'Yes.'

'But it wasn't her in Albacete, was it? And *someone* had to have been there.'

'Yes.'

'Was it the man, do you think? At Reception? It wasn't until I read the article that I realised, and...'

His sigh long, deep, he agreed, 'Yes, I thought so too. And you'd been talking to him, hadn't you? I'd assumed at the time that he was bothering you. I hadn't heard what he'd said, but on reflection——'

'You thought we were making arrangements.'

'Yes. I'm so sorry.'

'But it all seemed to fit, didn't it?'

'Yes, and over the years I've become extraordinarily paranoid about women following me; trying to use me. You were so like her, you see. Not to look at, but in little ways. Gentle and sweet,' he added with a sadly bitter smile.

'Maureen?'

'Mmm. And after reading the article it seemed so obvious that that was why you'd agreed to go to Albacete—to set me up. You came into my room... Do we have to talk about it now?' he asked thickly. 'I so desperately want to make love to you—in considerably more comfort.'

Desperately?

Helping her up, he took her hand and led her towards the bedroom. He eyed the narrow bed with disfavour, but climbed in anyway and invited her silently to join him.

My very own Svengali? she wondered. Yet even knowing that you were living in a fool's paradise didn't stop you from behaving like a fool. There were so many things she still wanted to know. But if she insisted on knowing now... Then he took the matter out of her hands by pulling her into his arms. The heat from his body distracted her, brought renewed desire—and she didn't want the moment spoiled.

As he wriggled into a more comfortable position, he caught his arm on the books piled on the bedside table. With a rueful smile, he picked them up in order to move them out of his way, then halted, stared at the top copy—and burst out laughing. 'Primers?' he exclaimed. 'Is this your bedtime reading? The cat sat on the mat...'

Her mouth pursed, she snatched them out of his hands and put them on the floor. 'Don't be ridiculous—and you don't need to read that,' she muttered crossly, trying to remove the piece of paper that had fluttered out of the books from his hand.

Holding it out of her reach, he glanced at it, and frowned. 'A list of your lovers?' he asked as he ran his eye down the list of men's names.

'No, it is not!' Seeing that he was not going to be satisfied with a glib answer, she explained reluctantly, 'They're in my reading class.'

'Reading class?' he queried softly, with a frowning glance at her. '*Reading* class?'

'The local library runs an adult reading class. I help out,' she muttered, not even sure why she was embarrassed.

Still watching her, a little frown in the back of his eyes, he handed the list across. 'People who can't read?'

'Yes. You can have no idea,' she began defensively, 'how wretched it is for people who can't read. They can't go anywhere, can't read road signs, traffic signs, railway stations...'

'I have a very good idea,' he argued. 'Are they mostly in their forties and fifties?'

'Yes.'

'Because as young men and women people are too embarrassed to admit they can't read, they practise ingenuity, learn excuses, then one day they wake up, realise how much they have missed, grab their courage in both hands, and pray for someone like you who will not laugh at them, who will help them. And I begin,' he added slowly, his face serious, 'to think that I'm getting out of my depth.'

Surprised, she asked, 'In what way?'

Shaking his head, he smiled at her with gentle warmth and wriggled himself flat. Turning on his side, he moved the quilt aside so that he could see her and began to smooth one large palm down her exquisite body. 'Helen said your leg was crushed,' he observed with some surprise as he reached her long legs. 'Apart from the scar on your foot, I've never noticed anything wrong with them. On the contrary, they're unmarred perfection.'

'Helen exaggerates. It was trapped, not crushed.'

'And your poor foot——'

'Don't touch it!' she warned hastily as he reached her ankle.

Startled, he drew back, and raised his head to look at her. 'Still painful?'

'Only if you touch it. The nerves haven't quite healed yet.'

'And there's nothing more painful than nerve damage, is there?' he asked sympathetically. 'Pain that hits without warning. No wonder you didn't want to scramble over damned cliffs.'

'No.'

'Poor old Jenna.'

'I expect it serves me right.'

'Mmm,' he smiled. 'If you will dive into wrecked coaches to rescue a parcel of schoolboys just as it's about to go over a ravine...' Breaking off, he gave a little shudder, and hauled himself up the bed. Taking her gently in his arms, he said soberly, 'You could have been killed.'

'Yes.'

'And the miracle is that you got off so lightly.'

She could be almost objective now, she found as she remembered that day. It was almost as though it had been someone else trapped in the wreckage, and she found that talking about it no longer hurt. 'I didn't even stop to think,' she murmured.

'No, just driving along, minding your own business,' he teased with a warm smile.

'Mmm; I naturally halted when I saw the crashed coach, got out to see if I could help. The teachers had got all the children out, or so they thought, then someone asked where Martin was...' Her eyes were wide, not really seeing Bay, just the crumpled coach and the boy still inside. Martin, Helen's grandson. Six years old. He'd been lying under one of the seats, unconscious, and she hadn't even stopped to think, just scrambled in, grabbed the boy, thrust him at the teacher, but before she could jump free herself the coach had lurched, tumbling her back inside, and finally given up its unequal struggle to stay upright. It had rolled down the ravine with her still inside. Blinking, coming back to the present, she smiled. 'Lucky.'

'Yes. Will you be able to dance again one day?' he asked quietly.

'I don't know. Maybe, in six months, a year—why are you looking at me like that?' she asked curiously.

'Because I don't understand you. Because I can't believe how wrong I've been about you. Because you don't seem bitter, angry. You're such a gentle soul...'

'Now why should I be bitter or angry?' she asked. 'To what purpose? I wasn't maimed, disfigured—all that happened happened because of my own involvement. I didn't have to climb into that coach... Anyway, it's not as if I was a prima ballerina, a famous tap-dancer; I'm a not very remarkable teacher in a small town. I have a great many things others do not. A loving family, a job that I love...'

'Are you really that philosophical?'

No, of course she wasn't, or not all the time, but whingeing never solved anything. With a little shrug, she confessed. 'I'm not very philosophical sometimes when it comes to the pain... but it could have been a great deal worse. I'm a very uncomplicated sort of person, you know. Boring, I expect,' she added, not deliberately probing his own feelings about her, or not entirely.

A slightly puzzled frown in his eyes, he asked slowly, 'Are you really what you seem? *Exactly* what you seem?'

Puzzled herself, she nodded. 'Yes, I think so. I don't think I need much to make me happy.'

'Blue skies and a smile?'

'Mmm, or even grey skies and a smile. All I need is to be warm, to be loved, to have an occupation, a roof over my head and enough money in my pocket to buy a dream,' she quipped lightly. And here was a man who sold them. Only, the dreams she wanted, money could not buy.

'I think...' he began.

'Yes? What do you think?' she prompted softly.

'Nothing,' he denied. His voice was slightly husky, the puzzled frown still in the back of his eyes. Then he smiled, pulled the duvet warmly across them, and began to kiss her again with slow enjoyment—until kissing was no longer enough.

It might be the most wonderful feeling in the world, she thought as she snuggled against him, to be held against a warm male body. To have smooth skin beneath your hands, a slow, reassuring heartbeat to make you feel safe, protected, but without the knowledge that you were loved as you loved the pleasure was dimmed. Love had crept up on her slowly, insinuated itself into her heart, her mind, without her consciously knowing that this or that was the moment it happened. Would it, could it be the same for him? Except that he hadn't realised it yet? He must feel a little of what she felt, mustn't he?

She made them something to eat around nine o'clock, and then they went back to bed, made love, slipped slowly into sleep. He woke her gently at just before eight the next morning by the simple expedient of blowing softly on her eyelids, and when she mumbled, twitched and reluctantly opened her eyes it was to see his warm smile. As she blinked up at him, seeing him already dressed, her heart contracted in fear. 'Are you leaving?'

'Do you want me to?' he asked gravely, but with the twinkle of amusement in his eyes.

'No.'

'Good, because I am merely going to retrieve my suitcase from the car.' Rubbing a hand over his bristly chin, he grinned. 'I've made the tea.'

'Thank you.' When he didn't move, she searched his eyes, and began to perceive fully what she might be letting herself in for. There were no real assurances, even when you both loved, but at least there was the assumption. With only one loving, there wasn't even that.

With a smile that felt forced, she asked, 'Get my robe for me, will you? It's hanging on the door.

He gave a wicked smile and shook his head.

'Bay,' she protested, half laughing, half embarrassed, and when he refused to budge she slid quickly out, practically ran to fetch it, and snuggled into its soft folds. 'Voyeur,' she scolded.

He merely grinned, and went off to retrieve his suitcase. Her smile died. This isn't going to work, she told herself. But how could she bear to lose him?

The next few days passed too swiftly. They toured the countryside as Jenna showed him all her childhood haunts: the cathedral at Wells; Glastonbury; Bath, where they solemnly toured the Assembly Rooms, the Pump Room and Roman Baths. They drove into the Mendip Hills, walked on the beach at Weston-super-Mare, explored Cheddar Gorge, and their nights were spent wrapped warmly in each other's arms. His previous life—Clarissa and his wife—was not mentioned, and Jenna, reluctant to introduce a sour note, did not ask.

Thankfully, her parents did not probe. Because what could she have told them? They would never have been fooled by a glib answer of friendship. They would know from her eyes, her demeanour that she loved, and he did not.

Three days later, without prior warning, at five o'clock in the morning, he woke her, and told her he must leave.

'Now?' she demanded in sleepy astonishment.

'Yes, my darling, now.'

And because she knew he did not love her she wondered if it was her fault. If she had said something, done something ... Frightened, and for pride's sake trying not to show it, wishing she could quickly clear the sleep from her mind, she shrugged into her robe and reluctantly accompanied him downstairs. What to say? What to ask? She wasn't *ready* for this!

In the grey light of the silent shop, he took her in his arms and gave her a warm, lingering kiss in parting. Not a hasty farewell, not rushed, she decided with a flicker of hope, but generous, warm. However, it didn't entirely banish the fear.

Staring up at him in the dim light, she felt a sudden little premonition that she would never see him again, and she shivered, clutched him tighter.

'Cold?'

'No,' she denied.

'I have to go up and see Mark. In Oxford,' he added when she only continued to stare at him. 'I try to see him every weekend in term time.'

Was it the weekend? She seemed to have lost track of the days. 'Oh,' she said inadequately. 'Drive safely, won't you?'

'I always do.'

'And give my love to Mark.'

'Yes. Take care of yourself,' he ordered softly. 'I'll ring you.' And before she could ask anything else he gave her one last swift kiss, turned, picked up his case, unlocked the door, and was gone. She heard his footsteps echo as he walked quickly along the street to where his car was parked. He had not said when he would be back. If he would be back. Only that he would ring. But of course he would be back. Something so special didn't end just like that. Did it?

Slowly locking and bolting the door, she returned to her flat. He would ring her. Of course he would. He'd said so. Maybe even be back Monday morning.

He didn't ring. Or write. And Monday morning came, and went. As did the next day, and the one after that.

CHAPTER TEN

WORRIED at first, then hurt, then angry, confused, Jenna's mood swung one way, then the other. No matter how hard she tried, she could not stop thinking about it; about him. It hadn't even been a week, yet she missed him so much. Every minute seemed like an hour, an hour a day, and no matter how many times she told herself not to be a fool it was as though part of her had died.

He'd made no promises, given no expectations—ony she had done that, tried to fool herself into thinking that it would be all right. And it hurt : o much! It hurt more than she would have believed anything could. Diversion didn't work! Hard work didn't work! She tried desperately hard not to take her pain out on anyone else, but it wasn't easy. She was short with her parents, short with her friends, overly critical of her students, of Anita who was trying hard not to let Jenna down.

She tried desperately hard to dredge up some of her former enthusiasm—to smile, laugh, be herself—but she couldn't. Everything seemed such an effort! And at night she couldn't even sleep for thinking about him, wanting his arms around her, his mouth on hers.

The weather got colder. Grey skies took the place of blue. And she wanted to seek him out, beg him to come back—it was so shameful.

Her parents wisely didn't comment on their daughter's behaviour. They ached for her, but knew that nothing they could say would help. And then, on the Monday, a full nine days after he had left, he came back. He leaned in the doorway, his face serious, solemn almost, his eyes steady. He looked tired.

Glancing at her daughter, who looked as though Medusa had passed in the last few minutes, then back to Bay, Mrs Draycott hastily excused herself.

'What's it to be?' he asked softly. 'A demand to know where I've been, why I didn't get in touch?'

And because her brain wouldn't get into gear, because she didn't know what to ask, didn't know what he wanted, she said stupidly, 'It's only been a week.'

'And did it feel like a week?'

'No,' she whispered. 'A year. Were you intending to come back when you left?' she blurted bravely.

'Yes. No. I don't know,' he sighed. 'Remember me telling you I was out of my depth?'

She nodded.

'Because up until then I thought it could be a casual relationship: meet when we could, when we wanted, friends as well as lovers, no commitment, no hassle. I thought either of us could walk away at any time without grief; thought you understood the rules. But you didn't, did you?'

'No,' she admitted almost guiltily, as though it were all somehow her fault.

'No,' he echoed, 'and I was too stubborn and stupid to admit that the rules no longer applied; that the game had changed—drastically. Can we go somewhere and talk? Please? It's important, Jenna.'

Important to whom?

He walked to the side-door, held it open and, mindlessly obeying, she walked upstairs. Going into the lounge, she just stood helplessly. He closed the

door, walked past her and went to stand by the
window, his back to the room. Staring at him almost
hungrily, she waited.

'When we were in Spain, why did you pretend to
be something you weren't?' he asked unexpectedly.

And because it didn't seem to matter any more, because not knowing that she loved him hadn't made
him stay, she explained quietly, 'Because it was what
you expected, because I thought it would be fun, and
because I didn't want you to know how I was beginning to feel about you.'

'Are you in love with me, Jenna?' he asked quietly.
'Yes.'

Turning slowly towards her, searching her lovely
face, he asked, 'Is it that simple for you?'

'Simple? No, it isn't simple, but yes, that's how I
feel. I knew you didn't love me, knew you didn't want
a commitment, but I couldn't bear to... I wasn't
strong enough to make the break myself.'

Leaning back against the window-frame, he pushed
his hands into his pockets, looked down at his feet
for a moment, as though gathering his thoughts. 'I've
been up at the house—the family home,' he explained, 'in Oxford, near to Mark's school. I kept it
on after our parents died and will keep it until Mark's
old enough to decide if he wants it or would rather
sell it. I thought he might need the security of knowing
it was there; a link with his past.

'Anyway, for the last few days I've been sitting in
the study, supposedly to work on a new book, only
all I've really been doing is doodling, thinking—
missing you. And I suddenly realised that I wanted
someone to be there for me... No,' he corrected
himself, 'consciously admitted that I wanted someone

to be there for me. Not an affair, driving off to meet with someone at a hotel, a flat, but *there* in my home. To be able to walk out into the lounge, see someone in the garden, cutting roses maybe, arranging flowers in the lounge, someone to smile, ask me how it was going... And I wanted it to be you. Knew I *needed* it to be you. Then I would tell myself it was stupid, irrational, that I didn't need anybody... But I did, Jenna,' he added with a painful smile. 'I did.'

Her heart aching, wanting to go to him, wanting to cry, she forced herself to wait.

'And once I had admitted *that*, I then had to be sure,' he said earnestly. 'This time I had to be sure.'

'Because of your first wife?' she asked quietly.

'Yes.'

Still feeling as though she was groping her way through a dream, a little frown in her lovely eyes, she asked, 'That article, it said that you threw her out; did you?'

'Yes.'

'With good reason?'

'Yes.'

'And Clarissa?'

With a twisted smile, he said, 'Everyone knew but me, didn't they? Mark knew and I wouldn't listen because it was—convenient to have her there, for her to keep an eye on him when I was working. He's a funny little chap—well, not so little any more...' A smile in his eyes, he continued, 'He usually tells me everything—what he's done, who he's met—and yet if it's an area that concerns my writing he——'

'Takes your creativity with pride and a determination not to have it dimmed by domestic disputes.'

'Yes,' he agreed with another faint smile.

'Because you must never be disturbed when you're working.'

'Yes. So I took Clarissa at face value, assumed, wrongly, that he merely resented having anyone else in the house who interfered in his own self-imposed jurisdiction; that it wasn't anything she had done, wasn't her in particular. None so blind as those who don't want to see, is there?' He gave a brief unamused laugh.

'And it was she who gave the rest of the information for the article?'

'To Maureen, yes.'

'And does she blame herself utterly?'

His smile widened, still a little sad, but wider, crinkling his eyes. 'Yes, because she said it was not meant, that she had no idea Maureen was so malicious...'

'Yes, she did; she said I was like her. Well,' Jenna qualified, fairly, 'she said I was *clever*, and the way she said it I assumed it wasn't a compliment. But to imply that I had deliberately seduced you in order to pass on details of your lifestyle... Why? Because she was jealous? Because she was in love with you herself and you never saw her in a romantic light?'

'No-o,' he denied slowly. 'I don't think she was in love with me. I think she looked on me as her property, and perhaps because once, for whatever reason, I'd told her I would never remarry...'

'She took the letter for the word? But why then tell Maureen about me? Tell her we were going to Albacete? Because it must have been her, if Maureen wasn't out there herself. And if Clarissa was so jealous of outside influence, so determined for you to keep your privacy, why on earth tell her about your lifestyle?'

'She said she didn't mean to, that Maureen kept ringing, asking to speak to me, and when I refused to speak to her she began asking Clarissa questions. And Clarissa got confused,' he said helplessly. 'Oh, hell, Jenna, I don't know how the bloody woman's mind works. She's gone and that's all that matters.'

'I suppose. How *did* you find out that it wasn't me?'

'By accident. I had to ring my publishers about something and my editor's secretary asked me if Clarissa had got the papers to me in Shepton Mallet, and said she hoped it had been all right to have told her where I was that first time I came here to see you. Now, I hadn't asked for any papers to be sent to me, so I was curious, because I had wondered, you see, how Maureen had known where to find me. So it all came out. Mark was there; he overheard the shouting; he was furious to discover how I'd treated you, and a few other little home truths emerged. So I came to see you.'

'Eventually,' she pointed out.

'Yes, eventually. And all the things about you that I denied feeling I felt. And the more I got to know you, the more complicated it got. I'd persuaded myself for such a long time that I didn't want any sort of commitment, any unnecessary clutter in my life—and you disturbed my concentration.'

'Did I?' she asked somewhat wistfully. Well, that was a bonus, wasn't it?

'Yes. I've treated you shamefully, disgustingly... I didn't mean to hurt you, Jenna,' he apologised quietly.

'And now?' she asked, so much pain and hurt in her lovely eyes that he winced.

'And now I want to make it right. Come here,' he ordered softly.

Was there a choice? No. Walking into his open arms, she rested her head against his strong chest, closed her eyes.

His cheek on her hair, he murmured, 'You smell of varnish.'

'Yes.'

'An adorable Huckleberry Finn: stained blue overalls, bare feet, and that ridiculous topknot. I missed you. Damnably.'

Her eyes filling with tears, she whispered, 'Did you?'

'Yes.'

'I missed you too.'

'Good.'

'Hated you,' she continued, 'was angry with you, with myself—miserable, hurt and aching.'

'Not so good.'

With a faint, reluctant smile, she looked up into his strong face. She wanted to push the tousled hair off his forehead, take the look of strain from his eyes; wanted to feel his mouth against hers. Dear God, she *ached* for this man. 'What happens now?'

'I take my courage in both hands and ask you to marry me.'

'Courage?' she breathed foolishly.

'Yes. You might say no. Ah, don't cry; please don't cry.'

'Marry me?' she gulped. 'When I don't even know how you feel?'

'Don't you?'

'No.'

'You should do.'

'Why should I? You never say anything to the purpose.'

'I don't?'

'No.'

He smiled down at her. 'You have absolutely no idea how extraordinary my behaviour has been towards you?'

Puzzled, she shook her head.

He gave a little sigh. 'My housekeeper thinks me the hardest taskmaster ever invented.'

'She does? I didn't know you had a housekeeper. At the house in Oxford?'

'Mmm. My publishers think I'm the most contrary, argumentative so-and-so ever sent to plague them. My accountant loathes me!'

'Oh, surely not.'

'Perfectly true. A veritable army of secretaries have found me impossible. My ex-wife took me for an easy option——'

'And learned her mistake?'

'Mmm.'

'Will you tell me? Now?' she asked quietly.

'I will tell you briefly,' he agreed, 'because I want so very badly to make love to you.'

That wonderful, terrifying, exquisite little dip in her tummy, she whispered. 'Go on.'

With a wry smile, hands smoothing her back—a delicious, warm, wonderful feeling—he murmured, 'It's not a story I'm fond of telling. I was twenty-four when my parents died, Mark two. Maureen was his nanny. To give Mark stability, we married. So quixotic,' he derided himself. 'She wasn't in love with

me, nor I with her, but I thought her warm and kind,
and I was grateful that she was prepared to give up
so much for my brother's sake. She could have remained in the house with him, stayed as his nanny—
there was no shortage of money; but in my naïveté I
thought that if we married it would give Mark the
stable base he needed. I put no pressure to bear on
her, didn't try to persuade her. We discussed it, and
agreed to marry. I thought we were both heart-free,'
he added.

'And she wasn't?' she asked quietly.

'Apparently not, seeing as she had an affair within
months of the wedding. It was a marriage of con-
venience, but not unconsummated, not uncom-
mitted—and if I hadn't come home early one day I
perhaps wouldn't have found out that she was
cheating.' His mouth twisted distastefully for a
moment, before he resumed. 'She thought I would
forgive her, that I needed her, for Mark's sake if not
my own. I didn't, and I wasn't prepared to argue the
matter. I don't forgive, or forget,' he added, his quiet
tone so very much more believable than anger would
have been. 'Not something like that.'

'So you threw her out.'

'Asked her to leave,' he corrected her.

'Insisted.'

'All right,' he agreed. 'Insisted.'

'And then?'

'And then nothing. I decided to bring Mark up
myself.'

'Because you wouldn't ask anyone else anything ever again? Any further offered help would
be spurned?'

His mouth twisted ruefully. 'Something like that. I was hurt, Jenna. I was also very young.'

Because she was a believer in people herself, she could understand his pain. 'I don't suppose it was easy, bringing up a little boy on your own.'

'No.' His expression lightening, he gave a funny little smile that endeared him to her more than he would ever know. 'But so very worthwhile. From the day he was born I adored that kid. Funny, aren't they—feelings? With Althea there was no bond of any kind, but with Mark, right from the word go, it was as though he were my son. I'd just finished university,' he explained, 'hadn't yet taken up an offer to carve out a career in the diplomatic service, so there was no reason not to look after him myself. There had already been enough changes in his young life and, as it happened, it worked very well. I *liked* looking after him. And when he started school, in order to keep myself occupied, I began to write. It was that simple. I don't know whether I was right or wrong, but——'

'Obviously right,' she smiled, 'judging by how he's turned out. And stop trying to fool me into thinking you have feelings of inadequacy, because I shan't believe you.'

His smile was crooked.

'And Mark clearly doesn't think you were wrong. And he certainly doesn't see you as you say your publishers and accountant do!'

A twinkle in his eyes, he said, 'No, because I behave to Mark as I behave to you, because I love him.' He watched her, and when her eyes widened hesitantly he nodded.

Still almost afraid to believe him, she said, 'He was afraid you would marry Clarissa. That she might trap you without you knowing anything about it.'

'Mmm, so he eventually said. She was a good research assistant,' he added fairly. 'With the added advantage of speaking fluent Spanish... Don't have any languages, do you?' he asked hopefully.

'No, 'fraid not.'

'Pity. If I hadn't been intrigued by Mark's description of you, concerned for his——'

'Moral welfare,' she put in with a quirky smile.

'Mmm, I would never have strolled so nonchalantly through your garden that first day.'

'But you strolled through first,' she remembered with a little frown.

A delightful smile in his eyes, he explained softly, 'Yes, because I knew he was intending to. He'd been watching you from his bedroom window; called me to see. From a distance you looked very young—sixteen or seventeen. It was a game, Jenna,' he confessed with a quirky little chuckle. 'He's changing...'

'Biological urges?' she teased gently.

'Yes. Sometimes a young boy, sometimes behaving as though we were the same age, desperate for recognition that he's almost a man. In Spain, whenever he saw a young lady that he thought attractive, he would call me... He likes my approval,' he added with a rueful grin.

'And so you came to see.'

'Yes. And discovered that you weren't sixteen.'

'And because I somehow reminded you of Maureen, was a—sensualist, you wanted to be sure that I wouldn't lead him astray.'

'Yes. And then he told me about teleporting; how you hadn't told him to shove off, as most people do, or ignored him, or patronised him. You'd amiably regaled him with nonsense, accepted him for what he was—a rather bored young man whose activities had been curtailed by a broken arm—and I hoped you were what you seemed.'

'But couldn't be sure because, Maureen aside, other young women had used him to get to you?'

'Yes. And because I was somewhat annoyed to find myself attracted to you I was harder on you than I would normally have been. And then, later, when the article came out, when it implied that you had—er—seduced me, I remembered your pose in that black swimsuit that revealed more than it covered, remembered you talking to that man in Albacete... I'm sorry,' he apologised, dropping a restrained kiss on her nose.

'But it did all seem to fit, didn't it?'

'Yes. Forgiven me?'

'Yes.' Because she'd allowed his assumptions to stand without explaining, yet more assumptions had been made, so he hadn't been entirely at fault. 'You really love me?' she asked hesitantly.

'Yes. I would have preferred your mother,' he teased gently, 'but, not wishing to break up a happy marriage, decided to settle for second-best.'

Staring up into his humorous face, wanting to touch him, press her mouth to that little indent beside his mouth, she asked drily, 'You cynically checked out the parents before pursuing your acquaintance with the daughter?'

'We-ll, you know what they say: see the mother and you see what the daughter will be like in a few years' time. I had no intention, you see, of putting my head in the same noose twice.'

'You didn't check out your ex-wife's mother?'

'No; a definite mistake on my part.'

'Mmm, foolish in the extreme,' she agreed, still sounding a little unsure of herself.

'I am sure, Jenna,' he insisted gently. '*This* time, I'm sure.'

'Are you? Our lifestyles are very different...'

'Does that matter so very much?' he asked gently.

'Not if you're sure.'

'I am. Will you come up to Oxford this weekend to see Mark? See the house? Decide if it's where you want to live?'

'Yes.'

'But before that we will go and see your local vicar, or registrar or whatever, and arrange a wedding.'

'You don't have to... I mean, if you don't want to marry...'

'I do want to marry. I do, Jenna,' he insisted. 'I can't think of anything I want more. I only hope...'

'What?' she asked worriedly.

'I'm not always the easiest person to live with. When I'm working, I tend to forget that people exist. I forget dinner engagements, birthdays, anniversaries...'

'I'll remind you,' she said gently.

'I might not listen...'

'Then I'll forgive you.'

His arms tightened and he groaned deep in his throat. 'Oh, Jenna...'

Her throat blocked by silly tears, she asked, 'Can I come with you when you travel? Do your research?'

'You won't be allowed not to.'

'I don't like flying,' she confessed.

'Then we'll go by sea. It's no problem.'

Staring up at him, she said wistfully, 'You make it sound so easy.'

'It is easy, and I think I'm to be congratulated on my quite excellent taste.' His voice was husky, his eyes dark as he stared down into her beautiful face.

'Congratulations.'

'Thank you. Say yes.'

'Yes.'

He gave a crooked smile. 'Kiss me hello.'

Standing on tiptoe, she raised her arms and linked them loosely round his neck. Her nose just touching his, feeling the tension in him, feeling her own, the way her body quivered, she kissed him on the mouth.

He kissed her back, hard, and Jenna closed her eyes and clung. Swinging her up into his arms, he carried her to the bedroom, laid her carefully on the bed. 'I'm glad you didn't believe the magazine article,' he said softly as he slowly began to remove his clothes. His hands shook slightly, she noted, and was comforted.

'Are there likely to be any more?' she asked thickly as she began to struggle out of her dungarees.

'Possibly.'

'But why *now*?' she asked, puzzled. 'It's over ten years since you broke up. And why on earth is she still following you around?'

'Because apparently bitterness makes one constant. And every time there's any press coverage about me, publication of a book, articles about my lifestyle, up she pops, determined to blacken my name, cause me grief or embarrassment. My success is apparently like a red rag to a bull—confirms her belief in her ill usage.'

'She doesn't think you were justified in throwing her out?' she asked in disbelief.

'Apparently not. She thinks I should have given her another chance. Then, of course, she would have shared in my success, instead of being convinced that I was the arbiter of all her ills. Here am I, apparently successful, fêted, rich, and there is she as she sees it—with nothing. Of course, we hammered out a reasonable financial settlement when we divorced, but she's convinced that I owe her something more, and if I won't pay up she'll continue to go to the Press, blacken my name. She's rather hysterical,' he said with a distasteful twist to his mouth as he continued to disrobe hurriedly. 'And presumably that was the only rag she could get to publish anything of late.'

'You thought I was like her...'

'*Thought*, Jenna,' he insisted. 'Thought.'

'I'm not hysterical,' she told him, just in case he should wonder.

'I know,' he smiled.

'Good. Foolish girl,' she muttered, her eyes riveted on his strong body, the smooth brown legs, hard-muscled thighs...

'Foolish? I don't think I would be so charitable. Trying to hurt me is one thing; if she tries to hurt Mark, or you, she will be very, very sorry.'

Jenna believed him utterly. For all his apparent amiability, she thought he would be a dangerous man to cross. 'Well, she'll get short shrift if she comes round here again,' she said with the air of having finished with that discussion to her entire satisfaction. Catching his hand, she dragged him on to the bed. Up until now, he'd been the instigator in their love-making. That was about to change.

'Not even interested, are you?' he asked in some amusement as he landed beside her, but she was pleased to note that his eyes were still dark, that his voice was none too steady.

'No—yes—it's nice to know *something* about you, but it doesn't affect how I feel, if that's what you're saying.'

'I suppose it is,' he agreed as he carefully framed her exquisite face with warm palms. 'You look like...'

'Huckleberry Finn—yes, I know.'

'A woman in love was what I was going to say.'

'Yes?' she asked huskily as that lovely warm pain spread to her tummy.

'Yes. Jenna,' he asked seriously, 'who's David? When I rang Helen from the complex to find out where you lived, after she'd told me about the accident, she said, "As if she didn't have enough trouble, that wretched David let her down." I didn't ask her, because it wasn't any of my business.'

'But it is now?' she asked softly.

'No, but...'

Brushing his thick hair off his forehead, she explained quietly, 'David was someone I was—fond of.' Not loved, because she hadn't known then what love was. 'We'd been going out together for a while, and I thought he liked all the things I liked, believed in the same things as I did. Then I found out he didn't. He was horrified by the accident, not because I might have been killed, badly injured, but because I'd been foolhardy, put him through a lot of anguish. He came to see me in the hospital, and he was *angry*; he said I should never have put him through anything like that...that I should never have got involved.'

'Understandable, if he loved you, was frightened of losing you.'

'No, it was more than that; it was as if I'd been *selfish*. I couldn't live my life worrying about doing things in case he disapproved...'

'So he went away?'

'Yes. And I was hurt, disillusioned... Then you strolled into my garden and he didn't seem to matter any more.'

'Good. And there will be no need for any more Davids. Because now you have me—and I love you.'

Such a simple statement, and it caused excitement and desire to spread along her veins, weaken her muscles. As she continued to stare into his expressive eyes, she asked throatily, 'Do you adore the very ground I walk on?'

'Utterly.'

'Oh, Bay,' she whispered. 'I never dreamed you would come to love me back. I can't believe——'

'Believe,' he insisted.

'I want to spend the rest of my life with you. Want to give and receive love and laughter.'

'Yes. Love and laughter,' he agreed, and then, with a groan, he lowered his head, held her impossibly tight. 'Don't listen to a word anyone says against me,' he begged thickly. 'Believe in me totally.'

'I will, so long as you love me.'

'I do, and if there's anything to tell I'll tell you myself.'

'If you remember,' she teased with a wonky smile.

'I'll remember,' he promised. 'For you I'll remember.'

MILLS & BOON

CHRISTMAS CRACKERS

A cracker of a gift pack full of
Mills & Boon goodies. You'll find...

Passion—in *A Savage Betrayal* by Lynne Graham

A beautiful baby—in *A Baby for Christmas* by Anne McAllister

A Yuletide wedding—in *Yuletide Bride* by Mary Lyons

A Christmas reunion—in *Christmas Angel* by Shannon Waverly

Special Christmas price of 4 books
for £5.99 (usual price £7.96)

Published: November 1995

Available from WH Smith, John Menzies, Volume One, Forbuoys, Martins,
Tesco, Asda, Safeway and other paperback stockists.

Christmas Journeys

4 new short romances all wrapped up in 1 sparkling volume.

Join four delightful couples as they journey home for the festive season—and discover the true meaning of Christmas...that love is the best gift of all!

A Man To Live For - Emma Richmond

Yule Tide - Catherine George

Mistletoe Kisses - Lynsey Stevens

Christmas Charade - Kay Gregory

Available: November 1995   **Price: £4.99**

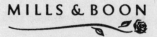

MILLS & BOON

WIN

A years supply of Mills & Boon Romances — absolutely free!

Would you like to win a years supply of heartwarming and passionate romances? Well, you can and they're FREE! All you have to do is complete the wordsearch puzzle below and send it to us by 30th April 1996. The first 5 correct entries picked after that date will win a years supply of Mills & Boon Romance novels (six books every month – worth over £100). What could be easier?

STOCKHOLM	PARIS	HELSINKI	ANKARA
REYKJAVIK	LONDON	ROME	AMSTERDAM
COPENHAGEN	PRAGUE	VIENNA	OSLO
MADRID	ATHENS	LIMA	

N	O	L	S	O	P	A	R	I	S
E	Q	U	V	A	F	R	O	K	T
G	C	L	I	M	A	A	M	N	O
A	T	H	E	N	S	K	E	I	C
H	L	O	N	D	O	N	H	S	K
N	S	H	N	R	I	A	O	L	H
E	D	M	A	D	R	I	D	E	O
P	R	A	G	U	E	U	Y	H	L
O	A	M	S	T	E	R	D	A	M
C	R	E	Y	K	J	A	V	I	K

Please turn over for details on how to enter ➡

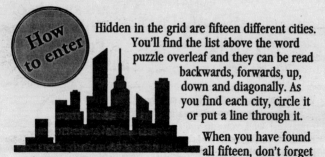

How to enter

Hidden in the grid are fifteen different cities. You'll find the list above the word puzzle overleaf and they can be read backwards, forwards, up, down and diagonally. As you find each city, circle it or put a line through it.

When you have found all fifteen, don't forget to fill in your name and address in the space provided below and pop this page in an envelope (you don't need a stamp) and post it today. Hurry – competition ends 30th April 1996.

Mills & Boon Capital Wordsearch
FREEPOST
Croydon
Surrey
CR9 3WZ

Are you a Reader Service Subscriber?   Yes ☐   No ☐

Ms/Mrs/Miss/Mr _____

Address _____

_____

_____ Postcode _____

One application per household.

You may be mailed with other offers from other reputable companies as a result of this application. If you would prefer not to receive such offers, please tick box. ☐

COMP495
D